A MOST ACCOMMODATING VICTIM

The medical report had attested what any layman who could bear to look would have seen with his naked eye: that the little bijou pistol had been fired only an inch or two from the nape of her neck. So he, or she, had been in the same room as Brenda; so he was probably someone whose presence had not unduly alarmed her; she had probably been talking to him at the time. So why had she turned round to enable him to shoot her? Had he played some puerile *What's that?* prank on her, and she had swung her torso? And his fingers had perhaps already been clasped round the pistol. He, or she, had held it an inch from her cervical vertebrae and fired.

Could it have been otherwise?

"Mosley and Beamish are an appealing odd couple as cops, both likeable human beings. If this is the beginning of a new series, may there be more!"

—*Washington Post*

Bantam Books offers the finest in classic and modern English murder mysteries. Ask your bookseller for the books you have missed.

Agatha Christie

DEATH ON THE NILE
A HOLIDAY FOR MURDER
THE MOUSETRAP AND OTHER
    PLAYS
THE MYSTERIOUS AFFAIR AT
    STYLES
POIROT INVESTIGATES
POSTERN OF FATE
THE SECRET ADVERSARY
THE SEVEN DIALS MYSTERY
SLEEPING MURDER

Patricia Wentworth

THE FINGERPRINT
THE LISTENING EYE
MISS SILVER COMES TO STAY
POISON IN THE PEN
SHE CAME BACK

Margery Allingham

BLACK PLUMES
DANCERS IN MOURNING
FLOWERS FOR THE JUDGE
PEARLS BEFORE SWINE
THE TIGER IN THE SMOKE

Dorothy Simpson

THE NIGHT SHE DIED
SIX FEET UNDER

John Greenwood

MURDER, MR. MOSLEY

Catherine Aird

HENRIETTA WHO
LAST RESPECTS
A MOST CONTAGIOUS GAME
PARTING BREATH
SLIGHT MOURNING
SOME DIE ELOQUENT

Elizabeth Daly

AND DANGEROUS TO KNOW
THE BOOK OF THE LION
HOUSE WITHOUT THE DOOR
NOTHING CAN RESCUE ME
SOMEWHERE IN THE HOUSE
THROUGH THE WALL
UNEXPECTED NIGHT

Jonathan Ross

DIMINISHED BY DEATH

Anne Morice

MURDER IN OUTLINE
MURDER POST-DATED

Murder, Mr. Mosley

John Greenwood

BANTAM BOOKS

TORONTO · NEW YORK · LONDON · SYDNEY · AUCKLAND

All the characters and events portrayed
in this story are fictitious.

*This low-priced Bantam Book
has been completely reset in a type face
designed for easy reading, and was printed
from new plates. It contains the complete
text of the original hard-cover edition.*
NOT ONE WORD HAS BEEN OMITTED.

MURDER, MR. MOSLEY

*A Bantam Book / published by arrangement with
Walker Publishing Company*

PRINTING HISTORY
*Walker Edition published December 1983
A Selection of the Detective Book Club, August 1984
Bantam edition / March 1986*

Bantam Books are published by Bantam Books, Inc. Its trademark, consisting of the words "Bantam Books" and the por-
trayal of a rooster, is Registered in U.S. Patent and Trademark
Office and in other countries. Marca Registrada. Bantam
Books, Inc., 666 Fifth Avenue, New York, New York 10103.

PRINTED IN THE UNITED STATES OF AMERICA

H   098765432

Murder, Mr. Mosley

One

'You are not contemplating,' the Assistant Chief Constable said, 'committing this to Mosley?'

Detective-Superintendent Grimshaw looked his master in the eye with a firmness meant to conceal the fact that he would rather have been looking almost anywhere else in the world. 'Chief Inspector Marsters is tied up with managerial crime—the Hartley Mason business. We've leave and sickness problems. Woolliams is looking after two divisions. Stout's going off on a course. And it *is* Mosley's patch.'

'But damn it, he couldn't even get to the scene of the crime.'

'He'd been up all night, sir: an epidemic of poultry-rustling over at Kettlerake.'

'Grimshaw—it will take Mosley until the middle of next year.'

'Oh, I don't know. He's good at talking to people—especially hill-folk. He *knows* everybody. They all like him—even when he's clapping his horny old hand on their shoulders. And we've got one here that has its roots well and truly in Mosley soil.'

'But have we ever let him loose within thirty miles of a murder before? Does he *know* that people sometimes kill each other? I'll grant you that when it comes to sheepdog-nobbling, cock-fighting and breaking into village halls—'

'Oh, yes, sir. In his thirty-four years in the force, Mosley has twice handled homicide—and in both cases he pulled it off. Once was back in 1954, when a man stabbed his wife in a Saturday-night domestic, and rang through to tell us he'd done it. I admit that he also complained about how long it took Mosley to get there.'

'And the second time?'

'A junkie on a camping-site, over on Back Moorside. He was leaning over the corpse with a dripping sheath-knife still in his hand, and a gang of Youth Hostellers cordoned him off and held him there as if they were photographing a still. Mosley spent two days satisfying himself that the chap wasn't being framed. That's what I like about Mosley: he's careful. And I'll keep a close eye on him, sir.'

'It strikes me you'd better gouge out an optic and attach it somewhere about his person. And Grimshaw—give him an up-to-date sergeant: someone who's heard about fingerprints and things.'

'Beamish, sir—on temporary transfer from Q Division.'

'Beamish! What's the betting they'll both have resigned from the force before the case breaks?'

So a cheerful-looking gentleman, who cultivated a shabby appearance and tried to seem older than his fifty-five years, arrived on a red service bus in the frontier village of Parson's Fold early one dusty afternoon in late October, after the scene-of-crime team had done all their work and departed. Parson's Fold ranks as a frontier village because it lies in that no-man's-land between Lancashire and Yorkshire where the county boundaries were changed early in the 1960s, and men had suddenly found themselves belonging to a neighbouring race which they had been brought up to hate from the cradle onwards. One local philosopher, interviewed on radio and asked how he felt about the change, said he did not know how he would be able to stand the climate.

Mosley travelled by bus because there had been a complex misunderstanding about the transport with which

Sergeant Beamish, fuming, was still waiting for him at Bradburn police station. Beamish did not know Mosley, except by improbable reputation, and was not yet in a position to suspect that the misunderstanding could have been an adroit piece of management on the old man's part.

Mosley went slowly straight into the public bar of an inn called The Crumpled Horn. It was against Section 178 of the Licensing Act of 1964 for him to consume intoxicating liquor on duty and equally illegal for the landlord to serve him. But the duration that he could spin out half a pint of beer made it a mild offence. He took off his black homburg, set it on a stool and leaned on the counter with his trenchcoat flapping open. Any buttons it had were concealed, and he never seemed to fasten these up, even in wet weather. And he looked round the faces of the lunchtime drinkers as if he were glad to see them all. What is more, they seemed equally glad to see him. Perhaps there was general local relief that the murder in their midst had been left in the hands of a man so unlikely to create anything unpleasant out of it as Jack Mosley. He leaned sideways on the bar, his blue eyes twinkling at Parson's Fold in general, his long strands of sparse hair swept untidily across his bald head and—as predicted—he talked to people.

An hour later, leaving a quarter of a pint of beer to be poured back into the ullage, he came out and sat in the weak October sunshine on the wooden bench round the oak tree on Parson's Fold's parlous patch of green, and wrote at very great length in his notebook, in the tiny handwriting that looked so peevishly pinched.

The trouble had started (as Mosley patiently reconstructed it in his notes) a month ago, early one dusty afternoon in mid-September, when there was sudden activity in the main thoroughfare of Parson's Fold, a street unreasonably named The Pightle. As far as Parson's Fold was concerned, activity meant (the movements of hikers, cyclists, botanists and fell-walkers excepted) any perceptible variation from the daily pattern.

On this particular day, the daily pattern had been moving inoffensively along its accustomed course. At two minutes past two, Bill Clitheroe's mobile stores had moved ten yards downhill, from outside Emily Cotterill's on the east side of The Pightle to Carrie Bowland's on the west. At three minutes past, a rook had flown out of one of the elms behind the Old Rectory, and at three and a quarter minutes past, it had flown back again. At ten minutes past old Arthur Blamire, widower, left The Crumpled Horn and crossed The Pightle to his cottage; at twelve minutes past he returned. Arthur Blamire was always nipping back from the pub to his empty home for a minute. He invariably had an explanation for his conduct—today it was that he wanted to put the kettle on for eventual tea. Such rationalizations, however, were never believed, and theories in the Horn were facetious, disrespectful and sometimes imaginatively obscene.

But now there came major aberrations from custom—one at sixteen minutes past the hour, and another nine minutes later, both involving motor transport, and both inspiring women to report to each other in their kitchens. Nor were curiosity and a sense of involvement exclusively feminine traits. The active cells in the brain centre of The Crumpled Horn all made postural adjustments enabling them to see out of the window.

The first arrival was a Mercedes-Benz, a car that evidently did not know its way about Parson's Fold. It performed a clumsy reversing manoeuvre round the oak against which Mosley was later to sit, and then parked askew and obstructively in the forecourt of the pub. Its driver came into the public bar, a brisk and blustering man in his forties, who scorned refreshment of any kind and merely wanted to know the whereabouts of Jackman's Cottage. There was a long silence, perhaps a quarter of a minute, whilst the herd mind decided whether to answer him; and then they all told him at once.

The second immigrant was a green MG two-seater, prewar to judge from its number-plates, yet clearly not an aficionado's car, though it could easily have been one. There was some buckling of the radiator grille, which an enthusiast would obviously not have left unattended, and the paintwork was scratched in several places under its patina of road-film. This was a vehicle that clearly did know where it was going, for it thrust its bonnet without hesitation up the alley that led to Jackman's Cottage, where its lady-driver got out, slammed its door and made a single unladylike comment upon the manner in which the Merc was blocking further progress up the lane.

She was an attractive woman in her mid-forties, with city-styled auburn hair, colourfully dressed in a green sweater that matched, perhaps, the original livery of her car, and corduroy slacks of a warm terracotta hue that went well with the knotted silk bandana that she wore round her neck.

'Inconsiderate sods!' she said, in a voice that carried down into The Pightle. She then entered the cottage, producing a key and opening the front door as if it belonged to her, and a minute or two later voices were raised, though not loud enough to be discernible to the forward reconnaissance elements that Parson's Fold had now discreetly deployed. They had not long to wait however for her to come out again, saying very angrily, and this time with a clarity that carried into The Pightle and beyond, 'And I tell you the house is not for sale.'

To establish which point she uprooted the estate agent's signboard and threw it petulantly into the long grasses of what had once been a lawn. It was seventeen years since anyone in Parson's Fold had set eyes on this young woman, but everyone knew who she was. Brenda Thwaites—as she was still thought of—was still rated an addled egg in Parson's Fold. And Mosley's memory went as far back as that. The year in which Brenda Thwaites had left home had also marked his promotion to detective-sergeant.

The brisk and blustering male followed her out of the cottage, attended by a woman in light tan suede who was evidently his wife. There was further conversation, which had to remain a mystery to the onlookers, but in which the man was evidently disbelieving what Brenda was saying. She seemed to have her way in the end, though, for presently the man began to upbraid her for placing her car where it was, preventing his exit from the alley. At first she seemed minded to leave it there, letting him stamp up and down until she had finished whatever business she had in the cottage. But then she thought better of this, got into the MG and reversed into The Pightle with a burst of querulous acceleration that had her wheels spinning in the September dust. Then, when the Mercedes had departed, she drove back to the cottage gate.

She was in there, silent and frustratingly beyond observation, for a full half hour. When she came out, she made sure the front door was locked, went and threw the estate agent's board even further out of sight in an over-grown herbaceous border. And then she walked down to the Old Rectory, where there was not a single native of Parson's Fold sufficiently courageous to follow her.

Inspector Mosley finished writing, looked at his watch—some of his superiors would have had their theories confounded by the fact that he had one—and made his own way up to Jackman's Cottage, a distance of some forty yards, which took him ten minutes, so many leisurely civilities did he have to exchange on the way.

Two

Jackman's Cottage was in fact a conversion, completed just before the outbreak of the Second World War, and achieved by throwing together four previous dwellings. It was built in the grey local stone and its original leaded windows had never been enlarged or modernized, so that the first impression was of austerity and hard living: the sort of home in which to face out the siege of a Pennine winter.

The garden had not been tended for a number of years. A profusion of sere Russell lupins and a population explosion of golden rod indicated where flower-beds had been. A roofed bird-table was broken and its plywood laminations had sprung apart. Near to it a gnome lay on his back, his nose broken and his colour bleached away, beside an ornamental stone trough whose water looked black under its green slime.

Mosley opened the front door with the key that Superintendent Grimshaw had handed him together with a large envelope of front-line documentation. He picked up the single letter that was lying on the mat—a credit card statement addressed to Mrs B. Cryer—and put it away in an inside pocket. It must have come by a very late morning delivery.

The interior of the cottage was as the scene-of-crime team had left it this morning: contents of drawers examined, likely objects dusted for fingerprints, possessions disturbed and put away again with a certain rough tidiness, even with respect, perhaps, but without tenderness. The outline where the body had lain was marked by a chalk-line. Mosley stood for a few seconds and contemplated it, ignoring it thereafter, unworried whether his feet obliterated it or not.

The furnishing of the home was such as a couple might have assembled who had married on a modest income in the early thirties—the beginning of the country cottage era in domestic interiors. A reproduction rural dresser, now losing strips of its veneer, dated back to that time. There had been one or two major replacements—a three-piece drawing-room suite from the utility years; that must have been bought when the couple had moved here from Bradburn, in a better though still vigilant state of affluence. And that had been, Mosley was well aware, in the mid 1950s. It was sometimes said of him that he knew everything and everyone in the twelve miles by twelve of moors, cloughs and valleys that were his territory—except, cynics added, the criminals. The rider was unfair, and the general proposition exaggerated: but he might certainly have been expected to know Arthur Thwaites, solicitor's scrivener in Bradburn since his boyhood before the First War, and managing clerk since the middle of the Second. Thwaites had been a colourless, industrious, unimaginative, meticulous man, well respected in Bradburn, and probably even more so in the almost absolute unsophistication of Parson's Fold. But not long after coming to this pasture, Arthur Thwaites had begun to suffer ill-health, had later died of a stroke, brought on, it was commonly believed, by the behaviour of that daughter who had come home in her MG a month ago.

The drawing-room furniture was not deployed as such. Sofa and armchairs had been pushed to one side, without regard for comfort or appearance and the main space was occupied by a three-quarter bed, still flanked by an invalid's side-table: a few bottles and pill-boxes—bismuth tablets, aspirin, a nasal dropper, a half-finished phial of oil of cloves—but among them no major prescriptions or regular doses. Mosley paid interested attention to the bed itself, turning back the coverlet, examining the pillows and holding a corner of sheet against his cheek.

He had known Nora Thwaites, too, Brenda's mother, who had married her husband at a time when there had seemed no likelihood of his ever advancing beyond the rank of a very humble pen-pusher indeed. Greenhill, her unmarried name had been, and she had come from a hill-farm some fifteen miles from here—a subsistence holding of the sort that is known as an intake: rough sheep pastures retrieved from the savage moor in a spirit of primeval and largely misplaced optimism. The Greenhills had been legendarily poor and her marriage to a man of letters—even the letters involved in merely engrossing conveyances for Fothergill, Fothergill, Foster, Sons and Fothergill—had been a rise out of class for her. She, too, had been ill for a long time. She had spent the last two years in a private nursing home. Then Brenda, the profligate absentee, had returned without notice after seventeen years and brought her mother back home.

All this Mosley knew, in a passive manner, which he had re-activated by laborious cerebration and quick reference before he left home to reams of his pinched-up writing in notebooks now decades old. His records of gossip were as rich as his talent for producing it.

Now he saw landmarks of his knowledge of the Thwaiteses' biographies in each room that he visited: a studio portrait of Nora Greenhill at the time when Arthur Thwaites had been courting her: in the late 1920s, it must have been, before Mosley had had any personal knowledge of the family. She was wearing fashions that dated from a few years before the photograph was taken: a characterless cloche hat and a shapeless frock from the age when women were disinclined to parade their femininity. It was a forced and unnatural Nora Greenhill, disciplining herself to face a camera in front of which she felt ill at ease, the end frustrated by the means. For Nora Greenhill had had the reputation of a certain wild beauty: the tangled, unconscious beauty of an impoverished girl brought up on a failed intake. She had rapidly lost it after marriage to a solicitor's clerk. There was one family group that occupied Mosley for a minute or two, dated about 1950. Arthur Thwaites was then in his early fifties, and at the apex of his career at law, the man who kept Fothergills, Foster and Company on the rails of office efficiency. Brenda was then a girl of about five—her parents had had her late in life—in floral patterned dungarees, her hair in a pony-tail. Her brother, twelve years older than she, was by now one of the promising fruitlings of Bradburn Grammar School. But Mosley knew relatively little about the boy, who had moved away into the world of redbrick university, a science degree and the mystique of industrial chemistry. He now lived in the Old Rectory, with a wife of whom Mosley knew nothing at all. There were no children.

Of Brenda he knew very little either—except what people said of her. It was true she had left home at seventeen for a marriage of which her parents disapproved, which they had declined to attend, but which their distaste for publicity had prevented them from legally opposing. It had surely been one of the shortest marriages on record, for Brenda—now Bryce—had got off the honeymoon train at an intermediate station, and was believed not to have been in touch with her husband again. An impetuous girl, people said, whose volatility led her into extremes. She had never returned home again until a month ago; and some said that this was because her parents had banned her. Her mother was believed to have been especially embittered, the more so because the girl had not even tried to make contact at the time of her father's funeral. She would probably have been rejected if she had—but this was not a logical sequence.

Certainly the characteristics of intransigence were latent in Nora Thwaites's face in the photograph that Mosley was now looking at: in her early forties, her figure gone and apparently not missed, her mouth turned down at the corners and her eyes resenting even the photographer.

What had happened to the girl after that rapidly stalled marriage? There were rumours. She had been spotted, so various claims went, in more than one Yorkshire or Lancashire town: Preston, Huddersfield, Heckmondwike,

Bolton—always too far away, and lost in too impersonal a populace for there to be any great danger of a direct Parson's Fold connection. There had been rumours of more men—of course. In her sixth-form days, even in school uniform, there had been a patent sexiness that had people forecasting ill for her. She knew what she had, and what it was for, and maybe was just a little impatient to be exercising it. But there had been more to her than just that, Mosley seemed to remember: standards, if that wasn't too sentimental a label. It must have been something that ran significantly counter to those standards that she had learned about her husband on that honeymoon train.

The most comfortable room in the house had been turned into a sickroom, and there was no sign that Brenda had made her private headquarters in the kitchen: she would not be the sort of woman who wanted her leisure dominated by reminders of domesticity. Mosley therefore spent a long time in her bedroom, which bore some witness to her previously acquired skill in bed-sitter home-making: the ability, for one thing, to keep unaesthetic essentials out of sight. Brenda Thwaites—Bryce—Cryer— had been no slut. Her underwear, mostly St Michael, was well kept and put away with fastidious tidiness. There was only one thing in her wastepaper basket—an empty ciga-rette packet of an expensive King Size brand. There were no stubs in her bedside ashtray, but the stains in it suggested a medium-heavy smoker.

The pictures that had been on the wall when she came back had been taken down and stored flat on top of the wardrobe: parental treasures—Cader Idris in mono-chrome and an engraving of a sentimental group in a Victorian smithy. She had replaced these by framed water-colours, originals, but with signatures which told Mosley nothing. They represented industrial scenes, but with extravagant, abstract use of colour. Her musical tastes were catholic, to judge from the sleeves piled by her record player, and ranged from Lindisfarne and Fairport Convention to Mozart and Stravinsky. Her current read-ing was a paperback Beryl Bainbridge and she also had Edna O'Brien, Susan Hill and Nina Bawden.

In a drawer Mosley found contraceptives in a sponge bag: a Dutch cap backed up by a tube of jelly of which about a third had been used. He unscrewed its cap and found the nozzle dried but not crusty. It might or might not have been opened within the last month.

He moved into the front bedroom, the one that must once have been parental territory, and examined the bed with the same lingering curiosity that he had given to the one downstairs. It was made up with freshly laundered sheets that had not been slept in. There was no sign that he could find of recent occupancy of the room. There had been a putting away of things, probably ages ago, a more recent skirmish against the dust—in general a banishment of life that amounted to positive coldness. Mosley sat down on a chair, motionless, as if punishing his memory, bludgeoning it to make it give him something. Then at last he took out his notebook and added one further line:

1972 to present? Eight years unaccounted for—not even rumours.

He put his notebook away, stood up and looked out of the window: nothing, really—only stone walls, slate roofs and a <u>passacaglia</u> of chimney-stacks and cowls. Suddenly a car came to rest outside and seconds later there was a hammering on the door. Mosley went down patiently and opened it, looking amiably into the eyes of a very angry young man: Sergeant Beamish.

Beamish was the sort of detective who believed in saliva tests and computers. He did not quite think that the colour of a man's socks could be deduced from a seminal stain, but he did believe that the ultimate assembly of silicon chips would leave the human brain ranking as candidly second-rate, its inferences amateur, its recall inefficient, its retrieval taxonomy haphazard. Intuition, of course, was a joke that no one any longer made, a synonym for guesswork and cheerful muddling through. He and Mosley had heard of each other, but they did not normally move in the same internal circle.

In addition, Beamish was an advanced democrat, who believed in the inferiority of age, experience and rank.

12

'Is this the way you treat all your sergeants?' he asked without inhibition. 'Leaving them conflicting messages?'

'Did I? I'm sorry: no harm done, at any rate.'

'Only time wasted. What have you found here? Anything that scene-of-crimes missed?'

'I don't know, really. Eight years of a young woman's life that need looking for.'

'Was there anything in the on-the-spot photographs? I believe there was some polaroid stuff for instant assessment. Anything preliminary from pathology or forensic?'

'I don't know. I haven't looked yet.'

Mosley nodded vaguely at the buff envelope which he had put down, still unopened, on a corner of the bed.

'I like to leave all that till I've made my own impressions.'

'Mind if I take a quick glance?' Beamish asked.

'In principle, do by all means. But there was rather an urgent job that I'd hoped you would do for me, if you don't mind.'

Beamish's lower jaw had already dropped, ready to parry the irony. But there was something in old Mosley's tone that made Beamish wonder whether it was intended as irony at all. He closed his mouth again, giving Mosley the benefit of the doubt—and incidentally, degrading the inspector a point or two in his assessment. Good manners at this stage of case-work could be a sign of muddled priorities.

'You'll find an estate agent's sign in the garden,' Mosley said. 'Go down and take note of their address. It's in Harrogate. Go over and pay them a visit. Find out who was given an order to view on September 16th. Go and see those people, whoever they are, and discover whether there is any personal connection between them and Mrs Cryer. I think we'd better call her that for the time being, to avoid confusion.'

'Yes, Inspector.'

'Oh, and Sergeant—if it's in some other force's territory, get all the necessary clearances and go and see them yourself. One always misses points when one tries to do things secondhand.'

'Yes, Inspector.'

'Even if it's at the other end of the kingdom,' Mosley said.

He let them out of Jackman's Cottage, locked it and tested the latch, then walked over to the Old Rectory with the gait of a Senior Citizen, clutching the buff envelope in his hand.

Three

The Old Rectory was one of those residences that must have tested the fidelity, not to say hardiness, of any Old Rector not blessed with a private income. Who could have afforded to maintain winter warmth in those rooms thirty feet square and fourteen feet high? Who could have attempted to populate those eleven bedrooms? Mosley walked up a drive beside a lawn that would have competed with an Oxford quadrangle for spirit-level immaculacy and freedom from weeds.

He could not think that he remembered anything about the woman that Donald Thwaites had married, except that she came from somewhere up in the Trough—Sedbergh or Settle—or was it from somewhere down in Ribblesdale: Balderstone or Roach Bridge? And young Thwaites had met her while doing his two years' national service, back in the fifties.

She opened the door to him, a woman well past the forty mark, of non-fat-making metabolism, a type for which the Greeks had had a word which Mosley had forgotten, as gaunt in temperament as in physical frame. She was very grave, though naturally unsurprised in the circumstances to receive a visit from a criminal investigator. The flat intonation and glottal stops of her native speech were variegated by a sincere but calamitous attempt at south country vowels. Although he did not go quite so far as this, Mosley was also on his most gentlemanly behaviour, and conducted himself as if he expected Beryl Thwaites to feel some measure of grief at the loss of her sister-in-law.

She led him through a wainscotted entrance hall decorated with patent brass-ware of the type that keeps its shine without polishing: pans, kettles, ladles, skimmers and warming-pans, none of which had ever been used—or designed for use. The Rectory drawing-room had been given an even greater sense of vastness by the addition of an immense picture window that looked out across the motionless autumnal valley to the dark hulk of Pendle Hill. The prospect combined magnificence with a strong innuendo of the elemental, greatly enhanced by the manner in which the garden of the house had been landscaped as a proscenium to the main set, clipped hedges and converging parallels of chrysanthemum beds leading the eye to the backcloth behind the elms. The room itself was contemporarily furnished, with shelving and wall-lamps by Habitat. Dangling fern-like house-plants interrupted the tiers of Book Society spines, and there were exhibits suitably illustrative of Donald Thwaites's profession: an early twentieth-century laboratory balance in its square-cut glass case, and a microscope with triple objective, likewise protected from dust and dusters.

Beryl Thwaites quickly gave the lie to the notion that she might be mourning for Brenda Cryer. She made a progressive statement, obviously rehearsed, and Mosley did not deny her the comfort of her preamble.

'I know, Mr Mosley, that it is wrong to speak anything but well of the deceased, and I know that whatever she may have done with her life, no one has the right to do what was done to Brenda. And I know that perhaps all along she was more to be pitied than blamed—'

'I am sure that this has been a very great shock to you,' Mosley said.

'To tell you the truth, Mr Mosley, it has been a long series of shocks from the very first moment that she arrived without notice and insisted on bringing her mother back home.'

Mosley nodded sympathetically, sitting uncomfortably in his chair, as if admitting that the quality of the furniture out-classed him. He had left his trench-coat and homburg in the hall and was now displaying a herringbone suit of the shabbiest grey with a silver watch-chain across his waistcoat and a blue and beige tie which seemed to bring out the worst in the ensemble.

'I mean,' Mrs Thwaites said, 'she could have written. She could have rung up. She could have come and talked to us. We had not heard a word from her for seventeen years, not us, not her mother, none of her old friends, not a soul. Donald and I can only think that she saw in some paper or other that the house was for sale and that she was worried about not getting her share.'

'But she did not apparently want the house sold,' Mosley said.

'No—and what a way of doing it! It did not occur to her to come down here and discuss it with us. She just tore down the sign, under the nose of an interested enquirer, and set herself up in there. And the next thing we knew, she had brought my mother-in-law out of the nursing home, had made a sickroom out of the drawing-room and was making the most disgusting exhibition of herself in the village.'

'How long since you had the old lady taken into the home?' Mosley asked.

'Two years, and I know what you are thinking, but you are wrong. We had discussed it, coolly and without passion, the three of us. My mother-in-law understood that there were times when her mind became confused, when she forgot things. She appreciated that it is beyond my resources to run two homes—I have this one to keep up for Donald; I have to entertain his associates. Also, she refused point-blank to come here and live with us—and I would be telling less than the truth if I pretended that I heard that with anything but relief. She did not see eye to eye with us about so many things. She agreed that it would be better for her to be where she could be looked after, with the companionship of people of her own age.'

'And she had enough funds to pay for this?'

'She had savings in the Co-op, something put by in the Post Office, a few thousands that Donald's father had left her, the proceeds of a life policy that she had held on him.'

'And all this was beginning to run out?'

'You must understand, Mr Mosley, that Donald and I never counted on being left anything by his mother.'

'Of course not. I assume that your husband is reasonably well off. He is a works chemist, I believe.'

'Chief works chemist. But that does not mean that he could afford the fees that the nursing home are now charging. Mrs Thwaites's capital was, as you say, diminishing—but the value of Jackman's Cottage has also risen absurdly. We believe it would make something like £35,000 on the open market, and, as I say, Donald and I have never reckoned in terms of a legacy.'

'Did you often go and see her in the home?'

'Weekly without fail.'

'Both of you?'

'Sometimes Donald went alone.'

'I see. And had Mrs Thwaites's condition deteriorated?'

'Very considerably. Sometimes she did not even recognize us. But in heart and limb she was remarkably sound for her age.'

'Yes, many of our old people are like that,' Mosley said. 'How well do you think that Brenda was able to cope with her?'

'Remarkably well. I was surprised. That, of course, was before the novelty of it wore off.'

'There must have been some sort of reconciliation between them. Was the old lady mentally up to that, do you think?'

Mrs Thwaites Junior allowed herself an apology for a smile. 'I would think that her clouded mental condition was the only thing that made reconciliation possible. She had never forgiven her daughter.'

'Did you see much of your sister-in-law over the last month?'

'We had her to dinner, of course. And we went over to tea at Jackman's Cottage on the second Sunday. Then I have to admit that things became rather strained between us.'

But Mosley seemed barely interested in this aspect, and offered no help towards continuing her line of thought. He waited.

'Brenda was difficult. She always has been—from the stories Donald has told me of when she was a child. And when she got into the upper forms of the High School—'

Mosley still waited. Perhaps Beryl herself had not qualified for High School.

'Well, as I say, Donald and I did our best to be sociable. But it took only a week or so for Brenda to be up to her usual games.'

Mosley disobligingly did not ask what they were. Beryl Thwaites paused for the drama of her next revelation to build itself up.

'Quite apart from extremely regular visits to The Crumpled Horn for bottles of gin, there were men,' she said at last.

Mosley continued to torture her with patient silence.

'I hate to have to tell you this, Mr Mosley—but in her own home village, returning ostensibly to look after her sick mother, she was receiving men at Jackman's Cottage before she had been here much longer than a week.'

Quite unexpectedly Mosley asked a question.

'And who were these men?'

Mrs Thwaites allowed her shoulders to twitch at precisely the right moment. 'Would you expect me to know? At first we thought it was only village talk—of which, I might say, there has been no dearth. But then Donald and I heard the cars come and go. Late at night. On one occasion someone stayed all night, not driving away until almost seven.'

Mosley did not seem shocked.

'Of course, I told Donald he must go and remonstrate. In a house that you cannot by any charitable stretch of imagination say belonged to her, and with her mother lying ill on a downstairs bed! We have our own position to consider, you know, with Donald expecting a seat on the board at the next AGM, and him a sidesman, and in the running for next vicar's warden. We are not exactly lords of the manor here, but people do look up to us. And I do think that we owe something to this house. After all, it was a Rectory. It has always had an aura as a centre of moral astringency.'

'And did he approach his sister?'

'He did.'

'What was her reaction?'

'She was outrageously and indecently rude to him. Wild horses would not drag from me the things she said to him about his relationship with me. Then, of course, we heard the rumours that my mother-in-law was no longer at the cottage—that she had been sent away again some-where. And we were the last to hear, even about that. That was what hurt.'

Mosley appeared to have dried up again as a source of guidepost questions.

'I can't describe to you what it was like, Mr Mosley, in a village like this, going into the post office or the grocer, knowing that all conversation will stop, and won't start again until after you've gone. It was the milk rounds-man, young Smethurst, who first circulated the story. He was in the habit of knocking at Jackman's, because Brenda was always forgetting to put out her order. And he usually put his head into the hall and shouted something friendly to the old lady. Then one morning, a week ago, he saw that the bed was empty—actually stripped of its linen. Being inquisitive, like all these country folk, he asked me, next time he saw me, where she had gone. And then the villagers started getting up to their typical ways and made excuses to go there, to find out what they could. Mrs Cotterill, the know-all of The Pightle, even went touting for laundry and mending—and came back telling people that she was sure that my mother-in-law was no longer there.'

Mosley continued to listen.

'Well, Donald asked me to go over, to save him from another intolerable scene with his sister. And Brenda was most insolent; obscene again. She showed me the bed, made up certainly, with the covers turned back at one side, but nobody in it.

'"She's in the lavatory, if you must know."

'And she went up and hammered on the toilet door, and she shouted, "Oh, Mother, how many times have I told you not to lock yourself in? I'll have that bolt taken off." Then she looked at me and said, "I don't suppose you've ever wiped her posterior." That, of course, wasn't the word she used.'

'How very distressing for you,' Mosley said; and raised none of the obvious supplementary points. Had she really fallen for a trick as shallow as that? Had she or her husband attempted no follow-up in the week that ensued? Hadn't her husband wanted to see his mother again in that time? Or his sister? Or were relationships between the two houses now beyond succour?

Mrs Thwaites allowed a tear to strain through into the corner of her eye. 'I did my best, I am sure, in an extraordinarily difficult situation. Of course, it is horrifying that anyone should have wanted to *kill* her.'

'*Did* kill her. I think it's possible she may have been in with rather a rum set of people,' Mosley said mildly.

'But it's the old lady I am worried about. I do hope, Mr Mosley, that you are leaving no stone unturned—'

'Oh, we have all the stops out,' Mosley said.

'Of course, I dare say she simply got tired of nursing her, after the first flush of madness. I've no doubt she's found some other home for her. But at least she might have told us. Mrs Thwaites *is* Donald's mother, and I could not bear to think of her being looked after somewhere second-rate. Still, I suppose until we hear something different, we must look on the bright side.'

'Invariably,' Mosley said.

The bright side? Brenda Cryer had been shot through the back of the neck, at an inch or two's range, with a bijou automatic of the kind that is known as a lady's handbag model in circles where ladies carry such models in their handbags. But the stops had indeed been pulled out—largely as county office routine—on behalf of Mrs Thwaites. Grimshaw had set that in motion and a little

21

cell of troglodytes, at a battery of telephones, were thumbing their systematic way through the Yellow Pages of an ever-increasing radius. But so far nothing had come in from a box-search of hospitals, private nurses and invalid homes.

Mosley went off again towards the nerve centre of The Pightle. He could honestly claim to know everybody who mattered—from his point of view—in Parson's Fold, and there was one man he was very anxious indeed to talk to. But that man was not at home; so, for the second time in one afternoon, he looked at his watch. It was evidently a keen sense of urgency that was impelling him. He knew from whom, in Parson's Fold, he could borrow a bicycle, and from that friend he now borrowed one. It was an emergency that he might even have been anticipating, for he drew a pair of clips from the pocket of his raincoat and fitted them round his ankles. With his coat flapping open and his homburg set squarely on the top of his head, he freewheeled down the hill out of the village.

Four

Mosley arrived at Murray-Paulson's in time to wheel his machine into the staff bicycle shed as the staff were wheeling theirs out; in time, too, to note that a large blue Vauxhall estate car still stood in the rectangle in the executive car park marked *Chief Chemist*. Otherwise, except for a small red mini in the space labelled *Company Secretary*, there was no indication of upper echelon life about the premises.

In a small way, Murray-Paulson's made paint: of very high quality and in custom-mixed shades. They were permitted to continue to do so in competition with the commercial giants, perhaps because their plant was so antiquated, their premises so dilapidated and their infrastructure so minimal that none of the giants was impressed by the viability of a merger. Donald Thwaites led Mosley through a laboratory reminiscent of a Dickensian blacking factory and settled them down in his office, a sort of minstrels' gallery overlooking his range of sinks, retorts, condensers and crucibles. Mosley, still wearing his bicycle clips, as if equipped for sudden flight if need be, maintained such dignity as was afforded by an adjustable armchair whose cushions appeared to have passed between the stones of a well serviced flour-mill. Thwaites's desk was a litter of paper-clips, promotional leaflets and routine analysts' reports on roneoed forms. His ashtray was that of a heavy smoker, and in it two filter-tipped stubs bore thick smears of lipstick.

Donald Thwaites was looking tired: it was not merely the events of today that had been nearly too much for him to handle. He had the nerviness of a man whose equilibrium had for some time depended on his ability to manage a peripheral picket of unmanageable women. Mosley, somehow omitting to mention that he had called at the Old Rectory, led him without passion through the events of the morning.

It had been the milkman, peeping through the letterbox, who had seen Brenda's body, at about a quarter to eight, when Thwaites had been within ten minutes of leaving for work.

'I ought to have stayed home all day, I suppose. But we'd a significant new contract at a critical stage, EEC stuff, and a working party was coming over from Duisburg to discuss consumer parameters.'

The scene-of-crime team had arrived at about a quarter to nine. At nine fifteen, Superintendent Grimshaw had come in from County HQ, looking with imperishable confidence for Mosley, and taking charge on the spot in his absence. He had organized a slow-moving queue for preliminary questioning. By a quarter to eleven, Thwaites was told he could go.

'I don't even remember your face among the officers who were milling about this morning.'

'No. I came late on the scene. Been up all night, you know. Serious wave of naughtiness going on, over at Kettlerake. You can't expect people to respect law and order if their hens aren't safe in their own back yards.'

Donald Thwaites nodded vaguely. He did not appear to see anything amiss in Mosley's juxtaposition of priorities. He was too far gone in general discouragement.

'Still,' Mosley said. 'What's in an hour or two? It seems to me it's taken the best part of twenty years to build up the situation in which your sister was killed. There's no point in wearing ourselves into wafers for the sake of five minutes.'

'I suppose not.'

'Your sister, now: one could hardly describe relations between you as cordial.'

'She was—shall I say?—difficult. Always had been. Even as a small child. We all spoiled her, her arrival being, well, late and unexpected. It seems improper talking about her like this, doesn't it? She was—well—difficult. Let's leave it at that.'

'Difficult in what way?' Mosley asked, relatively tenacious.

'She never seemed to know what she really wanted, and yet she wanted it badly. That doesn't make any sense at all, does it?'

Mosley expressed no opinion.

'I mean, at my wedding, for example, she was a bridesmaid. Very pretty. She was eleven. I was twenty-three. But she suddenly threw such a tantrum that she almost ruined the day for all of us. I know that she certainly did for Beryl. It was all about a spray of sweet peas that she didn't want to carry. They were deep maroon, and for some reason she'd pictured herself carrying light blue and lavender. She had preconceptions of what she wanted to look like, and she would not tolerate any variation.'

'Did she suddenly find, then, on a train, that this man Bryce didn't live up to her preconceptions?'

'Oh, Bryce! Bryce was a shyster. But he simply arose out of a situation. If it hadn't been Bryce, it would have been somebody else. My father even engaged a private detective, someone he knew through his office, to try to get a report on Bryce that might prove to her what he was. But it wouldn't have made any difference. If she hadn't found Bryce, she'd have found another—and it wouldn't have been anyone savoury. That wouldn't have suited her book at all.'

He looked Mosley in the eye. His own irises were tired and unhealthy, bloodshot, and occluded with yellow deposits of cholesterol in the corner veins. He lit a cigarette and drew in the smoke as if he depended on it for sustenance.

'I am trying to remind myself, Mr Mosley, that I

shouldn't be talking like this—but it's true. The trouble was compounded, I suppose, when she went into the sixth form at the High School. That was back in the early sixties: Beatlemania years. And I don't mean the music, though she was pretty far gone on that too: Freddie and the Dreamers, Manfred Mann, the Rolling Stones. She used to play it so loud in her bedroom that even the table the radiogram stood on was dancing. My mother and father nearly went <u>scatty</u>. But it wasn't only Merseybeat. It was rebellion: adolescent rebellion. There was nothing new in that, but somehow there was a nationwide cachet about it, a sort of universal cohesion—even a uniform. My mother and father were the last people on earth to understand it. They hadn't a clue what was going on in Brenda. I, in my time, had been orthodox, compliant. Even my work had been different, concrete and tangible, dependent on weighing and measuring. Brenda went on the Arts side, did History, French and Art at A level. She was reading Baudelaire when she was seventeen—and contemporary authors who left nothing unsaid. She went wild over painters like Warhol. She didn't hide her contempt for Parson's Fold and the values at home. She treated her father like an ignoramus and her mother like a mental defective. There was a teacher at her school in her last year, a girl just out of college, who fanned the flames of all this, fed her with every idea that was different and rotten. She was a terrible influence. Everything she said, every view she held seemed to be accepted without question. No: more than accepted—raved about. She had to go, a year or two later—the teacher, I mean—after a major row with the headmistress.'

Thwaites stubbed out a good inch of cigarette and immediately lit a fresh one.

'It was a domestic calamity when Brenda set foot in the house after school, or came in from an evening out. To make it worse, she had set her eyes on university, but my father could not see his way to finance her. He was a sick man. He had suffered from hypertension for years. He did old-fashioned copperplate handwriting, and you might say he had a copperplate mind. He knew he wasn't going to make old bones and he wanted to see her settled in something respectable, gainful and local before he died: secretarial, accountancy, local government or such. So there lay another bone of contention, and there was a flaming row every time either side of the question was broached. My mother, of course, backed my father's view all the way. She hadn't the remotest idea of anything that was going on in Brenda's mind, whether it was poetry, painting, politics or progressive pop. And by now, Mother had got the idea pretty firmly fixed that it was education itself that lay at the root of the trouble. Believe me, it was little short of civil war. I suppose in the normal run of things, Brenda would have got her university place and gone on independently; not that that would have done my father any good. It was commonplace security he wanted to see. But then Bryce came along.'

'And who was Bryce?'

'Someone she'd met at a pop concert—though they tried to make out that that was a coincidence: he was in some way different from the run-of-the-mill people you got at those places. In all fairness, I think there was a trace of truth in that. He was in his late twenties, at least ten years older than she; an artist, he said—sometimes. Sometimes he called himself a technical consultant. Sometimes he admitted that he was in advertising. In fact he was drawing hack technical diagrams for promotional material, over at Sinkers', at Goosnargh. And not very good at it, either, my spies informed me; holding precariously on to the job from one month to the next. But he had a red mini, and that was very dashing, twenty minutes after the school bus had gone, the village empty, except for faces behind curtains, and Brenda waiting alone by the oak for him to come revving down The Pightle. He was a collector: that's what I told her. "He's a collector," I said. "And you're the next specimen he wants in mint condition in his album." And she laughed—she could be insufferable— "I'm already in his album," she said. "And I'm a collector, too. Only I keep mine in slide-out trays in a glass cabinet."'

'Collector or not,' Mosley said. 'He was prepared to marry her.'

27

'Well, he might have done worse for himself, mightn't he? She was attractive, she was witty, she had ideas of her own. She could have made him an interesting home. Outside the family circle, I dare say she could even be agreeable for hours at a stretch.'

'So why did she abandon him on a train?'

'Your guess, too. They were flying from Manchester to Tenerife. She said that was bourgeois, but not as bad as Torremolinos. She got out twenty miles from here. Maybe he had said something that made her see the light suddenly. She was no fool: only blindfolded—by herself and that silly chit of a teacher.'

'And didn't he ever come back here? Didn't he try to trace her through the family?'

'Never. I don't think Sinkers' tolerance had much longer to run. And maybe he pictured us Thwaiteses coming down from the hills fanning our hammers.'

He was capable of humour, then; but this was an isolated example of it.

'And Brenda?'

'We heard in a roundabout way that she was sharing a flat and had taken a factory job—assembly line stuff— somewhere in North Yorkshire: Rangate.'

'You didn't go to see her?'

'To be laughed and abused off the premises?'

'There was never anything between you that one could have called friendship?'

'Inspector, unilateral friendship is an uphill furrow. Brenda was only seven when I was doing my National Service. She was eleven when I came down from university. We never got to know each other. And if we are going to be here much longer, Mr Mosley, I would like to phone my wife.'

'By all means.'

Mosley watched his face closely as he did so: the uneasiness, the frown—the shock when he realized that his wife had already been questioned.

'You didn't tell me that you'd already talked to Beryl.'

'Didn't I? I apologize. I assumed she'd have rung you. Now: do you mind if we change the angle a little, Mr Thwaites?'

'Does it matter whether I say yes to that or not?'

A midge-bite, rather than a wasp-sting: which Mosley did not even bother to slap.

'When did you last see your mother?' he asked, suddenly—and apparently unconscious that he had just uttered an inane and tasteless epigram.

'I suppose it would be about ten days ago. But I gather you have already had all the relevant information from Beryl.'

'I would like to hear your account.'

Thwaites did not actually wriggle, but he looked as if he would have liked to.

'I admit it must seem curious to you—but you must understand, Mr Mosley, that the circumstances are not normal—they have been abnormal with us Thwaiteses for years. It isn't a question of love, Mr Mosley—it's a basic absence of communication. Three quarters of the time my mother doesn't recognize me. When she does, the chances are that she will mistake something I say—or impute to me something I haven't said. Then she'll become insulting, obstreperous. She lives in a twilight world, and even when she acknowledges reality, it is a reality that moves without reason from present into past, from ancient history into sick fantasy. They call it senile dementia. I tried to handle it on a charitable family basis—and if I had gone on, it would have broken my home. My wife has tried very hard—but she lacks that common ground that remains from my boyhood years. Even after Brenda brought Mother home, we tried again—had the pair of them to dinner. I need hardly tell you that it was catastrophic.'

'And that is the state your mother was in when you put her into the nursing home?'

'That is how she was beginning to be. What would you have had me do, Mr Mosley?'

'I am not accusing you, Mr Thwaites.'

'No. I am accusing myself—I suppose. Beryl is always taking me to task for it. She says I am too soft-shelled.'

'Your sister must have been surprised by your mother's condition.'

'I know Brenda too well. At first she would refuse to

accept it, refuse to believe it. She would see only what she wanted to see: just as she saw only what she wanted to see in Charles Bryce—until suddenly the truth caught her like a wet towel across the face. I tell you, I know the way her mind works. That's why I'm not as worried as you might think I ought to be about where Mother is.'

Mosley looked at him with hopeful enquiry.

'Brenda isn't unloving, unkind. She is obstinate, self-deceptive. She is an intellectual and aesthetic snob. She identifies with wrong-headed minorities to the point of perversion—'

All in the present tense—though by his own account, all his evidence for this was nearly twenty years old.

'She rides rough-shod over people's opinions; only her own beliefs count. But she's not totally irresponsible—not in the material, the humane sense. She wouldn't do physical harm, and she wouldn't see physical distress in a situation where she could relieve it. I am sure that she has sent Mother somewhere to be looked after—perhaps only on a temporary basis, to give herself a rest. Perhaps she even only wanted to clear the house as a rendezvous for one of those men who keep coming.'

'Somewhere private,' Mosley suggested. 'We, of course, are covering all the public institutions—all those that are advertised or registered.'

'She wouldn't send her back to The Towers,' Thwaites said. 'That's one thing I'm certain about. I know Brenda too well. She'd never repeat history: that would be the abnegation of progress. That would be admitting us right and herself wrong. I know she'd try something new.'

'Could she afford to, do you think?'

Thwaites shook his head, disclaiming knowledge.

'She did her best to get it over to me that she's not done badly for herself. She was contemptuous of what I earn—and though I say it myself, I am doing quite comfortably.'

He looked down into his sub-standard laboratory, with its ancient brown woodwork, its stained benches and its sense of improvisation and archaic methodology.

'I know this doesn't look much, but the firm is flourishing, and the board knows it all starts in here. It would have to be a big offer to tempt me away. But Brenda looked down her nose at me. She may have been exaggerating, but she gave the impression that she'd been moving in circles that didn't think small over money matters.'

'But she gave you no idea of the nature of those circles?'

'None whatever.'

'Or of whether she had come away from them permanently?'

'She gave no hint. There was an aura of something, a suggestion that it would have been tampering with unstable dynamite to have asked. But surely, though—'

Thwaites paused, indecisive. Mosley got him to continue by simply raising one eyebrow.

'Surely that's what it's all been about—all these cars in the night—the bullet in the back of the neck. Doesn't it show that she was still as thick with unsavoury circles as ever she had been?'

'She may only have thought she'd escaped,' Mosley said, barely audibly. 'Well, Mr Thwaites, I know you are wanting to get home. I am sorry to have detained you so long. There's just one little thing—'

Thwaites had shown immediate relief at the suggestion that the interview was over. The anxiety returned to his eyes at the hint that some venomous question had been held in reserve.

'Did your mother suffer much from toothache?' Mosley asked.

'That's strange. Of course, she couldn't. She'd none of her teeth left to ache. But she did complain sometimes. I wondered if it was like the patient who has a pain in a leg that's been amputated. Or perhaps there was something amiss in her gums. But whenever we vaguely suggested getting her to a dentist, there always seemed to be a miraculous improvement.'

Mosley nodded. His face seemed to suggest that this slotted in neatly with views he had formed. He did not say what they were and gave the impression, not rare among strangers who had to deal with him, of being unable to clear his mind of irrelevant trivialities.

Thwaites saw him through the laboratory, across the factory floor and out by a side-door that opened directly on to the car park. As they passed the administrative suite, Mosley was aware of a door slightly open, where he would have expected it to be closed: *Company Secretary*.

And from the staff bicycle shed, as he tested the state of his tyres with his thumb, he saw a woman watching him from one of the ground-floor windows: a middle-aged woman, not saved from dowdiness by artificially blonde hair quite out of keeping with either her age or her heavy, plum-coloured costume.

Five

It was well advanced twilight by the time he was leaning his machine against the rose-trellissed porch of the modest country villa. Some of the residents had already been put to bed. Others were sitting round the walls of a day-room either watching or dozing through a moderately moronic television panel game: old ladies with their hair sticking out at the sides in ludicrous tufts; old ladies clutching the handles of their knitting-bags as if they suspected every other inmate of being a potential snatcher; old ladies staring unresponsively at the screen; others staring at nothing.

It was a good nursing home as such places went, which is to say that it did not waste money on extravagances, even on some of those extravagances that patients' relatives believed they were paying for. But an honest effort was in reserve for emergencies, and physical discomfort was alleviated where it could be. Mosley fortuitously knew—it was odds on that he would—the retired SRN who came in to help with the bedtime rounds. She was a woman to whom he would have committed the care of himself, if he had needed it.

Nellie Palmer put him in a corner of the small cubicle used as a nurses' common room, furnished him with a cup of gut-tanning tea and left him to catch up with his note-writing until she had delivered the evening pills. Tags and ends of patients' quarrels drifted in to him: 'You go back to your own place, Kathleen Darwent. This isn't your corner.' And now and then Nellie's voice was raised in final judgement. 'Lizzie Armitt, you're old enough to know better.' Lizzie was eighty-eight.

Nellie Palmer came into the ante-room at last, carrying a cup of tea for herself. She was a woman of Mosley's own age-group, with kind eyes, brisk movements that made short work of work, and a lack of hesitation, even in snap decisions. She was a woman who had been involved on the edges of a great deal of suffering and stupidity—and had once or twice been plunged into the maelstrom on her own account.

'Nora Thwaites?' Mosley asked.

'We were shattered when that daughter came for her. And shattered when we heard what had happened to *her*. I suppose they've got you on it now.'

Mosley blinked.

'I'll give that girl her due. I know all that's been said of her, but she was shocked when she saw the state that her mother was in—shocked and angry.'

Mosley looked at her expectantly.

'It's that glazed look,' Nurse Palmer said. 'They all get it. I've seen them come in here, and for the first day or two they wander round talking to those who can't get out of bed, trying to show friendly. But within a week they give up. Then you see them sitting, looking at a wall—or out of the window at the roses and squirrels—and not seeing them.'

'Is that how she spent the last two years, then—with the glazed look?'

'Nora Thwaites was a mutterer. She muttered.'

'Muttered?'

'To people who weren't there: her son and her daughter and her daughter-in-law mostly. Always spiteful, always complaining, blaming them for putting her into situations that were unfair and inhuman.'

'How did she behave when they came to visit her?'

'They? There was only the son—he came alone after the first two weeks. I respect that man, Mr Mosley. He

34

scarcely ever missed a Saturday afternoon and sat loyally
through his hour, no matter what mood she was in. She
sometimes begged and screamed and demanded for him to
take her home again. But most often of all she just ignored
him, wouldn't look his way when he sat beside her,
wouldn't even eat cake for him at tea-time. There were
times, of course, when she didn't even know him—or
mistook him for somebody else.'

'Who, for example?'

'Mostly for one of her own brothers, as a matter of
fact—and he was a man that she didn't care too much for,
either.'

Out in the ward someone moaned loudly. Nellie
Palmer cocked her head on one side, but decided that it
was not a case for intervention.

'I remember once,' she said, 'that he had another
woman with him. I don't know who she was. Can't have
been too close a friend of the family, because she wouldn't
come in. Just stayed out in the car, reading a magazine,
while he sat out his hour.'

'What sort of woman? Can you describe her?'

'Nondescript. About his age. Shapeless. Unattractive.'

'Relative of his wife's, I wouldn't wonder,' Mosley
said. 'What I'm really wanting to know is about old Mrs
Thwaites. What was the true state of her mind?'

'It's hard to tell. She had better days than others.
They all do: me too. You ask my opinion: I'll give it you. I
think Nora Thwaites knew more of what was going on
than she ever let be seen. Some days, of course, she was
not with us at all. On others, I'm pretty sure she knew
where she was, why she was here—and just how hopeless
it all was.'

A fresh cadenza of moaning broke out and Nellie
Palmer got up and went out to the sufferer, treating her
woes as if they were an offence by a naughty child.

'Be quiet, Gladys Bretherton, and let the others get
some sleep.'

She came back to Mosley.

'Of course, you know, these people in here are all
crafty, far gone though some of them are. In places like

this little things are apt to loom large—like if there's half a slice of bread and butter over. And Kitty Spencer has got my jam, Nurse, the little jar Mrs Gilman sent in for me. They jockey for pathetic little advantages. They think themselves into situations where people are being unjust to them—and then use all the guile they can muster to get the tables turned. Sometimes we pretend to give way to them, let them win a round—as a bargaining point, I might say. Some of them have an irrational confidence in some drug or other—maybe nothing more startling than aspirin. Others take against a medicine they've been prescribed and will go to great lengths to get out of taking it.'

'And that's a general picture of Nora Thwaites, all the time she was here?'

'Not entirely. As I say, there were days when she knew who we were. You would see her eyes come unglazed, and she'd sit looking round at people, weighing them up—and hating them.'

'So what was the reaction when Brenda came for her? Did she know her own daughter?'

'We wondered what was going to happen. I might say, there were two or three of us at action stations in the wings in case of major upset. But it all went off quietly. Yet it had not been one of Nora's good days. And she didn't actually say anything, not a word, when she was taken into the office and confronted with Brenda. We'd brought her in in a wheelchair and she sat, oh for minutes, not looking at any of us, especially not at her daughter. Then she did glance at her, didn't smile, didn't speak, but somehow we got the message that she'd grasped the situation and wasn't going to create a scene. Of course, I didn't hear what Mrs Lumley said to her in the office after Brenda had gone. But still she didn't show any feelings, any joy, any bitterness—not even curiosity—when we eventually helped her into that bashed-up green sports car and the wheels crunched up the drive. More tea?'

Mosley said no, he would have to be going, and began tucking his notebook into his already bulkily overloaded inside pocket.

'There was one other thing, Nellie.'

'Oh, yes?'

'Can you tell me whether Mrs Thwaites ever suffered from toothache?'

Nellie Palmer gave a throaty little laugh.

'She did, yes—oh, I suppose about every six weeks or so. She had complete plates, upper and lower, and I looked two or three times to see if there was an abrasion, but there was nothing that I could make out. We'd give her an aspirin and she seemed to forget it. But there was one time when she nagged about it for two or three hours, and we told her we'd arrange for a dentist to come in and give her gums the once-over. The very thought of it seemed to cure her.'

'And the whole thing was forgotten about?'

'She didn't complain any more. We get very used to imaginary symptoms in here, Mr Mosley.'

He unleaned his bicycle from the porch and tested his lamps. The front one gave the sorriest flicker and the tail-lamp no sign of life at all. He pushed the thing philosophically out into the darkness.

Six

'Why,' the Assistant Chief Constable asked, 'has Mosley sent Beamish to Edinburgh?'

'Largely to get him from under his feet, I would imagine,' Detective-Superintendent Grimshaw said.

'I always hate asking for a clearance when it's already a *fait accompli*. I take it we can put up a reasonable case on paper?'

'On paper. In point of fact, I'd probably have done the same thing myself. The house-hunters that Brenda Cryer disturbed happen to be living in Scotland at the moment. Mosley wants to know how fortuitous the connection is.'

'Ten to one entirely fortuitous,' said the ACC. 'And what is Mosley himself doing, if anything, at the moment, do you think?'

'Going through several thousand pages of journal—I hope.'

'Journal?'

'Mosley keeps a daily diary—has done since he joined the force in 1946. He puts down everything that comes his way—everything he hears, everything anybody believes, any rumour that's current or public reaction that's seething. It runs to several hundred school exercise books, all carefully numbered. He does the index on Sunday mornings and his rest days. I might say that I don't know, officially, that the thing exists. If we as a force kept records, especially in this age of computers, of individual foibles of no criminal significance, the *New Statesman* and such would lose their marbles. But I see no harm if a private individual wants to do it for his own amusement. And I've been grateful for Mosley's journals more than once.'

'I do believe, Grimshaw, that you're actually glad you have no one but Mosley to assign to this case. And now there's something else. Chief Inspector Marsters: when are we going to get him back into general duty circulation again? I must say I'm finding it difficult to nail him down on his actual progress in this Hartley Mason business.'

'I don't like the smell of it either, sir. But if only a quarter of what Marsters suspects is true, it's something we've got to face up to. Managerial crime—'

'I know. But I wake up sweating cold in the night, dreaming that Marsters has overstepped it. We mustn't have overkill: and yet we either ram it home or leave it alone. Hartley Mason is a partner in the most respectable firm on this flank of the Pennines. Old William Fothergill would turn in his grave at the slightest hint of what Marsters believes.'

'I know, sir. But Mason isn't one of the family at Fothergills. And one does hear rumours from time to time that there are some in the family boat who don't care for him.'

'Rumours, Grimshaw! I'm sick and tired of rumours. You're getting as bad as Marsters.'

Mosley could not remember her name, but he did know the approximate date and, strong-mindedly steering past fascinating digressions and forgotten side-tracks, he finally put his finger on a sub-paragraph headed: *Farrington, Sandra.*

Sandra Farrington had come to Bradburn High School in September, 1962, straight from college, supercharged with a brand of sociology distinguished mostly for its indignation, of which she had assimilated mainly the slogans, and which she had had the pragmatic sense to suppress during her interview with the Governing Body. She it was who had become Brenda Thwaites's mentor during that last year at school, at a time when the girl, utterly disillusioned by everything she saw, at whatever level she looked, might possibly have lacked the resolution to assert herself, had she not seen confirmation of even her most whimsical rebel ideas mirrored in this deliciously anti-authoritarian figure, who nevertheless spoke, because she was a teacher, with the voice of formal authority.

Mosley, picking his way through his pages, located Miss Farrington at the stage, a year or so later, when she had walked off the Speech Day platform in protest against the positively elitist ambitions of the headmistress's report. The headmistress, no less of a pragmatist than she was, had skilfully provoked Miss Farrington over the next few months, to the point at which the girl had resigned, rather than waiting to be dismissed: which might have brought trouble from her professional association. And although politics, ideologies and religion may not be considered when making appointments to the public teaching force, it was remarkable with what consistency over the next few months she lost posts to other candidates when she applied for work with neighbouring authorities.

So she got married—the *so* was Mosley's interpretation in his pinched pothook notes. She got married to a man called Francis Dereward Tudor Balshaw who, whether or not he initially shared her views on the vices of the establishment, was nevertheless for remunerative purposes the promising executive servant of a monopoly that traded according to accepted market practices. He was on a month's notice, with a preferential company mortgage on a house of nicely gauged prestige. His young wife had to respect company rituals if she wished remuneration, mortgage and prestige to continue. Mr F.D.T. Balshaw became effectively anchored. Mosley wondered which of the conflicting elements in his wife had prevailed.

There had been no more diary entries about the Balshaws after 1965, but after false runs through the telephone directories of several dormitory conurbations,

Mosley finally ran them to earth on a large open-forecourt estate south-west of Rotherham.

He went there himself. Beamish had telephoned a negative report, and was now heading south though still north of the border. Mosley, dismissing his taxi out of sight of his destination, entered the open-forecourt estate, not turning aside to ruminate on its vandalized almond trees, its up-and-over garage doors or its wrecked telephone kiosks. The avenues were named after culinary herbs, the closes after gastrophiles. It was in Escoffier, leading off Marjoram, that he came to Evenlode, the domain of the Balshaws.

The garage doors were up and over, and in the space beside their second car he spotted the electric mower and plastic lawn-sprinkler that were all part of Sandra Balshaw's linkage with the bourgeoisie. He also noticed, from their car-stickers, that they had been to Interlaken, Dubrovnik and Antibes.

And Sandra was mercifully at home, now a buxom woman of—yes, he had it precisely—thirty-seven, in denim slacks, a woven leather belt and hair entirely concealed beneath a double triangle of printed nylon. She seemed embarrassed at having been caught unprepared—and at first surprised at the nature of his interest.

'Brenda Cryer—I've seen her name in the papers, of course. A horrendous case. But of course, I know nothing at all of the woman.'

'But as Brenda Thwaites?'

A furrowed brow and some seconds of internal rummaging were needed before even that produced an echo.

'She's not the same one! Well, fancy my knowing her! Well, hardly knew her, of course. Just one year, with me on one side of the fence and her on the other. Yes: I do remember her—just. But I don't know in what way I can possibly help you. She was a kid in her last year at school, and I was a kid in my first year beyond the pale. I only *taught* her—or was supposed to.'

There were ornamental beer steins from Munich and Mittenwald, a straw donkey from Fuengirola, a reproduction Aristide Bruant poster and any number of small silver cups and trophies for badminton.

'You didn't ever hear from her again? You didn't correspond?'

'Heavens, no! I wasn't that sort of teacher.' She laughed at the incongruity of the conception. 'The less said about my teaching career, the better. I didn't influence anyone.'

'In that case, I don't think I need take up any more of your time.'

'I did meet her once after we both left the place, though.'

Mosley clapped his hands together once, and left her to talk.

'Before Francis and I were married—just before. He was working at Rangate, in the North Riding, at Brooker and Ponsonby's, and I'd gone over to be taken out to lunch. And I saw her—well, I wouldn't have recognized her: it was she who saw me. She was coming out of a factory, with a whole host of other girls, all in beige nylon overalls. "Miss Farrington!" she shouted to me across the street, and I had to stop, and she expected me to know who she was, and I didn't. And when she told me, at first I couldn't remember. Her name meant nothing to me at all. And then, when it gelled, I could hardly believe it. She'd been quite an attractive girl—immature, but full of vivacity, reaching out, looking for something, as I suppose we all were in those days. But now! Well, the one thing that struck me most about her was the smell. She was working in a small concern—not one of the major suppliers—that made brake and clutch linings out of some sort of fibre. It stank sickeningly. It clung not only to her overalls, it must have been deeply absorbed in her pores. She was wearing no make-up, and looked as if she had been sweating all morning. She had lost flesh and the haggardness of her face gave her a mean look that I didn't associate with her at all. Her fingernails were misshapen and dirty and split, and her hands—she had slender fingers— were oil-stained and chapped. We only spoke for a minute or two. I was late for my date, and she told me there was a small caff she wanted to get to—she even mispronounced it like that, deliberately, I think to underscore what she'd come down to—a caff, that she wanted to get to before the barm-cakes ran out. That was the one thing that most sticks in my mind—her aggressiveness, a sort of outlandish enjoyment, a perverse pride in the mindlessness of the work she was doing—and the equally mindless company that she was stuck with. I remember thinking to myself: is this why we teach them Keats and Mallarmé, why they learn the law of diminishing returns and the memoirs of Tocqueville and Engels? And that was the last I ever saw of her, Mr Mosley, from that day to this.'

'I suppose you'd even have difficulty telling me the name of the firm she was working for?'

'What would you expect? I saw its signboard once, fifteen years ago. I doubt whether I even read it then. But I'll tell you what—' Her expression brightened. She would help if she could. 'Francis will know. He drove daily down that road for two years.'

'When will he be home? I'll ring through.'

Seven

So there was nothing more to do that day, and it was D + 2 before Mosley could get up to Rangate. And first there was Beamish to pacify.

'I might say, Mr Mosley, that our Scottish colleagues would have been only too happy to pull that chestnut out of the fire for us—or, rather, let us know by return that there was no chestnut.'

'No, well. It's happening all the time,' Mosley said cheerfully.

'Not to me. Not in my own division, it isn't.'

'No, well. Better luck next time. I have in fact another little chore for you, if you would be so kind.'

'Kindness itself,' Beamish said, in a tone whose implications, he feared, went unnoticed.

'A question, then: when is the toothache not the toothache?'

'When it's ajar?'

Something was happening to Beamish. He thought it might be the onset of madness.

'Put it another way, then,' Mosley said. 'If a woman with no teeth complains of toothache, what does it amount to?'

'Hypochondria?' Beamish tried.

'Could be, but I think not. Mrs Thwaites, Senior, has no teeth. She also consistently has toothache. She had it at home, before she went to the nursing home, she had it in the nursing home itself, and she had it at home again after her daughter had brought her back. On her bed—side table at Jackman's Cottage I found a half-used bottle of oil of cloves. And as she'd hardly be rubbing that into her dentures she must, I surmise somewhat uselessly, be rubbing it into her gums. Now what does that suggest to you?'

Sergeant Beamish at least appeared to be giving it some thought.

'Delusion,' he said at last.

'I think not. I think an uncut wisdom tooth—which is not my imbecilic idea of a joke. A lot of people suffer from them—including seventy-odd year olds. Probably it has become impacted into the bone, and ought to have been taken out years ago. But Mrs Thwaites appears to have developed a fear of the dentist. Perhaps she had a rough time when the last of her molars made way for her dentures. The merest suggestion of dental attention produced a false relief, of the sort that I believe is called psychosomatic.'

'So?'

'So Mrs Thwaites comes to live with her daughter, who is far too strong-willed to let her mother get away with dental cowardice. Old Mrs Thwaites has to be sent away to have the thing attended to—perhaps doesn't even know where she's being taken. But it's a rotten bit of oral surgery at any age, and definitely not so good in your seventies. It needs a general anaesthetic, probably stitches afterwards, and a few days' recovery time. So Brenda Cryer gets two birds with that stone. She gets her mother attended to—and clears the deck for the man who is coming to murder her. Which is where you come in.'

Beamish did not look as if he thought that a stimulating chore was about to be handed to him.

'Find the dentist who extracted Mrs Thwaites's impacted wisdom tooth, and find out where she was sent to convalesce.'

'I may have to ring every dentist in the United Kingdom.'

'It would take just as long with a computer,' Mosley

said unprovocatively, 'by the time you had programmed it. But I'll tell you this: I'll bet Brenda sent her mother to her own dentist, the one who last treated her. So you'll not only find the old girl—you'll discover where Brenda was living before she came back.'

'It will still be a long job,' Beamish said.

'I expect you'll find some way of narrowing it down. What's the word everyone uses these days: a rationale?'

Mosley's next visit was to Superintendent Grimshaw's office, where he cast a typescript down on the desk. After thirty years' experience, Mosley still typed as if the order of letters on the keyboard was a constant source of surprise to him.

'Well—that's out of the way.'

Grimshaw looked at him for one second as if he might, after all, be delivering a miracle.

'Kettlerake,' Mosley said. 'Hens. Thirty of them.'

'Thirty hens, Mosley? That is a substantial contribution to the division's loot-retrieval sheet.'

'Thirty hens mean a lot,' Mosley said, 'to five families who keep half a dozen each.'

Only then did he set out for the North Riding.

Eight

Rangate was a grey and rectilinear desert of trading estate: soft drinks, non-ethical drugs, baby buggies, mixed pickles and office sundries. It was possible to see the factory one wanted, its signboard impudently challenging a couple of streets away, and still not be able to find the right combination of intersections. There was not even a challenging signboard, however, for a well-spring of brake and clutch linings, because this no longer existed. It was after all fifteen years since Brenda Cryer had last sweated out her working day with the brake linings entering into her soul through her pores. Passers-by hurried on, unwilling to protract conversation with this middle-aged imbecile whose secular happiness seemed to depend on the discovery of a dried-up source of malodorous fibres, no longer on the estate map. Mosley stood and contemplated the asymmetrical wilderness of staff car parks—the Spruce Greens, Venetian Reds and Daytona Yellows—and reflected that even if he found the concern in its full, evil-smelling productivity, his chances of pinpointing the Cryer connection were necessarily slight. But any other approach must surely promise slighter hopes still, and he was never one to be put off by considerations that others found impenetrable. He asked a security guard at a frontier-post, a Pakistani dustman and an old woman with a grandchild in a pram. And he finally learned from a council surveyor with a theodolite that the firm had been taken over at the height of its prosperity, dismantled and sold as a development site before the laws against asset-stripping had been strengthened.

Mosley stood in the middle of the road, abused by lorry-drivers leaning out of their cabs. He looked, idly at first, at a group of girls in mob caps and nylon overalls of imperial purple, who were just coming out of the gate of a factory that provided a portion of the world with its requirement in fishermen's floats. He hurried over to speak to them, earning further opprobrium from a cylindrical load of newsprint whose approach took him unawares.

'I wonder if you could tell me if there's a caff anywhere near here where a man could get a barm-cake?'

They were an uproariously happy bunch, raucous, uninhibited and made-up in a variety of styles suggestive of latter-day sirens: Mosley noticed that most of them were young married women. They heartily begged him to accompany them, and he toddled along with them—*toddled* is an apt word for his gait in their sprawling company—with a great deal of shrieking laughter, the apparent implication being that one or the other of them—perhaps even an *ad hoc* alliance—was going to rape him before they arrived at their destination.

Amid this invigorating escort he arrived in a very few minutes at an older part of the settlement, the nucleus of the original village, which possessed a church, two pubs, a war memorial, a mobile fish and chip shop and a small bakery, round which other cohorts were gathered in nylon overalls of clashing hues. Connoisseurship of barm-cakes, a yeasty type of roll, apparently demanded that they be eaten hot from the oven, and the parturition of the midday batch at this establishment had been timed to a nicety for years. The small loaves were cut laterally in two by the consumer, and served as vehicles for sandwiches either of potato chips, or of thick slices taken from the interior of a pork pie. Thus lunched the young working married women of Rangate.

Mosley was patient. And eventually, from management and assistants more intent on purveying barm-cakes than on helping improbable policemen with their enquiries, he came away with the single piece of material information that the one person between Trent and Tees most likely to help him was Jessica Makepeace. He also carried away with him a variety of unsolicited views. The common thread that ran through them all was that Old Jess could be difficult, even dangerous to handle.

It was well into the afternoon before Mosley had run her to earth—a wispy, wiry and shrunken woman in her seventies, who for the inside of her lifetime had been a supervisor at Crawleys. Yet her spirit had not been exhausted by long years of handling fights, jealousies, strikes, sit-ins, handbag and cloakroom pilferers, husband-thieves and boyfriend slanderers. She scanned Mosley's features in a manner that confirmed the tales he had been told of her: her intolerance, her singleness of mind, the indestructibility of her opinions once formed. What was odd was that after that first moment of terrifying assessment she seemed to take to Mosley. And Mosley took to her. It was as if two soul-mates had suddenly discovered each other, their common ground a shared view of humanity. Old Jess put her kettle on within five minutes of Mosley's entering her house.

'Brenda Bryce? I remember her. And she's the same person as this Brenda Cryer—?'

Mosley reconfirmed the truth.

'I remember her well. One of the best workers I ever had. Such a good worker that at one time I thought I would have to get rid of her.'

Mosley's eyebrows requested expansion of the paradox.

'It was a disruptive influence, you see, having someone on the shop-floor who actually seemed to be enjoying the work for its own sake. It upset people, having someone there who was not trying to dodge the column all the time.'

'It seems to have been anything but enjoyable work.'

'That's the whole point. It was revolting. I remember one married couple who broke up because the woman, who worked for us, wouldn't change her vest before she went to bed. If her husband happened to wake in the night, the smell made him have to get up and vomit. She said she'd tried most things, and this was the best kind of birth-control she knew.'

'And this was the kind of company in which Brenda Bryce took pleasure?'

'Not exactly. I can't say she ever made a friend here.' Jessica Makepeace used *here* as if she were still working for the firm. 'There were all sorts of upsets, not because she couldn't get on with people. It was because they wouldn't get on with her. The work was a sort of drug to her: something she was hooked on. You see, you could tell, right from the outset, that she was a young woman with something that had to be put far behind her. I don't mean something to forget: it was some experience stronger than that, something she had to wipe out by a sort of personal self-violence. Hard work alone wouldn't have done it—at least, I don't think she thought so. It had to be rotten, stinking, soulless work, in rotten, stinking, soulless company. It was as if she'd put herself on trial and come up with a sentence of penal servitude on herself, the only thing that would clear her. It was obvious to anyone who looked at her for twenty seconds that she was a girl who'd gone through something—something not to her credit: but perhaps a good deal less to her discredit than what she was tormenting herself with. I didn't ask questions. In my job, you learned not to. The answers came to you—if they were going to.'

Old Jess had no cakes to offer, and her idea of afternoon tea was thick and thickly buttered slices, cut from the loaf and served up with jam from the jar.

'And all the time she was here, she was working like a steam-engine, trying to qualify herself for something better. Evening classes: shorthand, typing, accounts, even company law. There was not an evening in the autumn and winter when she hadn't a class of some sort or other, and the study she did on the side was nobody's business. I used to ask her why she didn't ask for a transfer to our own office—I could have fixed that for her in a jiffy—and then she'd have had better company and a chance to get in some practice with typewriters and things. But she had the idea—and I think after all she was right—that if you went in at the bottom, that's where you were likely to stay. The way to the thin end on top of the pile was to go in at the top—not try to clamber through all the opposition inside. Besides, with the piece-work rates she could get here on overtime, she was better off on the floor than she would have been at a desk. She was saving like fury, hardly spending a penny on herself.'

'Things might have been set fair for her, then.'

'Are things ever set fair for anybody? I think she had more staying power than any other girl of her age that I ever came across. But that wasn't enough.'

'She didn't stay the course?'

'She took the exams at the local college, but she said that was still not good enough. She'd been saving like mad—to get to London, for a year in a private residential college, a place with a name, something to juggle with. Her argument was that if she went there with the back of the work already broken, she'd have every chance of coming out on top. She was going to be satisfied with no less.'

'She had her eye on a top job?'

'I don't know quite what it was that she pictured— right-hand woman to a cabinet minister, something like that, I imagine. An indispensable: one of those who do all the real work—and have all the real influence.'

'In other words, she thought big.'

'But not beyond her capacity. Brenda could have gone on to big things. I always said so.'

'And obviously, you were closely in her confidence.'

'No.' Jessica Makepeace was categorical on the point. 'On one evening, and on one evening only, she loosened up and talked to me. We'd had one of our shop-floor crises, but a worse one than usual—and as usual she'd been at the centre of it, through no fault of her own. It all happened because it had leaked out through someone in the office that she had A levels—something she'd always kept dark from the others. When that word went round, you'd have thought she'd spent the last eighteen months boasting about her intellectual superiority, whereas in point of fact I've seen more swank in a school-leaver with one CSE on his record. But this triggered off something that was just waiting to be detonated. They accused her, not only of giving herself airs, but of coming in where she didn't belong, of stealing some other working girl's employment from her. They hated her for being different, even though she never laid claim to be. And this time she was terribly upset about it, that was what took me by surprise. She was in such command of herself in all the other difficulties she'd hemmed herself round with. And here she was, looking as if she was going to go under—for something that, candidly, didn't matter a damn. I asked her round here for an evening—something I've never done before or since for one of our work-force. And that evening, just for once, she talked to me. She needed to.'

Somewhere behind a lifetime of keeping brake and clutch linings in production, Jessica Makepeace had come from a family home, with her favourite radio programmes, cinema memories of the thirties, albums of holiday snapshots. There were framed portraits of relatives about the room: uninformative, unoutward-going faces, each with its secret range of aspirations and disappointments.

'That's how she came to tell me about her marriage. We knew, of course, that there'd been one, because she always wore a ring. That, I think, was all part of the self-torture—a reminder. Also, it did at least make some casual men think twice before bothering her. I don't think she told me the whole of the truth: only part of it. I don't know how much you know about Brenda's background, Mr Mosley?'

'It would be safest to assume I know nothing.'

Old Jess looked at him with a sudden shaft of suspicion.

'If you are putting me through some sort of test, Mr Mosley—'

'I am not.'

And, oddly enough, she accepted that without further question.

'She'd got married too young to some man her family didn't approve of. I never did hear her call him by his first name. And suddenly, on the train, not an hour from home—they were on their way to the Canaries—she

52

caught sight of him, from an angle, and suddenly asked herself, what had she done. She couldn't explain it, she knew she just couldn't stand him, couldn't bear to be tied to him for life. The way she put it, he was suddenly, shockingly, sickeningly the same as everyone else. So she simply got off that train, and never set eyes on him again. Myself, I think there must have been rather more to it than that. Something must have triggered it off. But that's how it went. Once her mind was made up—for no matter what slender reasons—I mean slender from the ordinary person's point of view—nobody was going to unmake it for her. Unfortunately, I believe she'd be obstinate to the point of silliness, rather than give way. I'd a long talk with Brenda Bryce that evening, Mr Mosley, and though I thought she was silly in a lot of ways, I had great admiration for her.'

'But she went on and kicked over the traces again?'

Jessica Makepeace refilled their tea-cups: a rich, orange brew, that would have gladdened the heart of Nurse Palmer.

'The little bit of bother in the workshop settled down, as these things always do. The women found some other way of relieving their boredom. Brenda took her local exams, came to the end of her evening classes, didn't register for any new subjects, and I began to think it wouldn't be long before she told us she'd be moving on. But the trouble was that she felt pretty flat with her studies behind her. Her evenings were empty. The pressures were off. Someone, some girl at the next bench, tried to persuade her to come to a works social, and to everyone's surprise Brenda said yes, it was time she moved in on a fresh world. She went to that social, and met a man there. And that, Mr Mosley, put an end to a lot of big thinking.'

'You mean,' Mosley said, 'that she went off with him? Did she get a divorce? Was he a married man? Did she leave the district? Did she shack up with him, here or elsewhere?'

'I can't tell you a thing, Mr Mosley. She gave in her notice, worked it out, went away.'

'Where did she live, here? Flat-sharing?'

'She had various living arrangements while she was at Crawleys. It took her a long time to settle down. She had the same sort of difficulties in digs as she had in the factory. In the end she came to some arrangement that lasted. She shared with two or three other girls. But they weren't ours, and I've no idea where you would find them.'

'In Rangate?'

'Somewhere the other side of the by-pass, that's all I can tell you.'

Beamish laboured under persistent difficulties. He was a man who still had to stabilize his attitudes, both towards others and himself; but he was no fool. The nagging suspicion had already formed in his mind that his assignment covering the dental records had something in common with his trip to Edinburgh: it was a way of getting him off Mosley's shadow. But he also had a persistent niggle that there might be more than a molecule of sense in it. The dental explanation was a hunch on Mosley's part—but not unfeasible. If it were true, then the man who broke it could be within a step of breaking the whole case—perhaps even of breaking it before his own inspector could reach the scene. Sergeant Beamish therefore applied himself with characteristic industry to a survey of dentists.

It was, at first contemplation, a discouraging prospect. The Yellow Pages listed two hundred dentists in this region alone, some of them working in partnerships, which meant multiple records. He hopefully considered the fact that the list of dental technicians was shorter, but it was by no means certain that new dentures would have to be made after the extraction of a wisdom tooth. Maybe some time would have to elapse before the old lady's gums were ready for a new fitting.

Then Sergeant Beamish remembered something from his own last visit to a dentist. There had been a form to fill in before treatment could be started, and it had had to go to some kind of executive council for ratification.

Beamish turned from the Yellow Pages to the directory proper and there, after a number of false trails, he found the number of the Area Dental Officer, who was able to put him on the right track. He began a more viable round of telephoning.

The degree of helpfulness and alacrity of response varied, but three quarters of the way through the morning he struck a clerk who actually turned up the name of a Mrs Nora Thwaites on an index-card: in East Yorkshire, somewhere along the coast, in a large village north of Scarborough.

He checked—not that he needed to—that Mosley was still away from HQ; and he went to see Grimshaw. Beamish's contempt for those set in authority over him extended to Grimshaw, but he kept that opinion to himself. Grimshaw, whether by his just deserts or not, was a power in the land.

And Grimshaw looked at him with close interest. Could it be that in their so far slight association, Mosley had already taught Beamish something?

Grimshaw listened with diplomatic appreciation to Beamish's account of his dental researches, which did not omit reference to the acuity of mind that had put him in touch with the executive councils.

'So what you are suggesting is that I should authorize you to go off on your own to some Yorkshire fishing village?'

'I am quite sure that it would be Inspector Mosley's intention for me to follow it up at once, sir.'

'It is equally possible that he might want to follow it up for himself—where *is* Mosley, by the way?'

'Rangate, sir.'

'What the hell is he doing in Rangate?'

'I don't know, sir. He didn't say.'

'Or when he would be back?'

And Beamish made the most of it. 'The impression I gathered, sir, is that Rangate might lead him even deeper into Mrs Cryer's past.'

'It might be fatal to underestimate Inspector Mosley's sense of direction, Sergeant.'

'I am sure, sir.'

'I think perhaps you had better go as soon as you can to Ember Bay, Beamish. See if you can locate Mrs Thwaites. See what state of mind she is in. See if you can find any trace of Brenda Cryer in the locality. See what she was up to up there, and if possible get the colour of her local associates, without talking to them too much, in case you cut across any ploys that Mosley might have going.'

'Yes, sir.'

'And report by phone direct to me, if Inspector Mosley is still not available, the moment you have something concrete to offer.'

'Sir.'

The relative density of his use of that word had never been so great as within the last five minutes.

Nine

Beamish enjoyed driving to Ember Bay because of the mental processes that accompanied the journey. It was a reasonably safe bet that the murder of Brenda Cryer was connected with the circles in which she had been moving just prior to coming home. And even if these were unconnected with the immediate vicinity of Ember Bay, there must have been some correspondence between her and the dentist who had treated her mother, something that would put him safely on her trail. Moreover, the dentist was almost certain to know where the old woman had been taken to convalesce; and that would almost certainly be in some place where even more vital information about Mrs Cryer would be forthcoming.

Mrs Thwaites herself, of course, was a more dubious prospect. The general picture was of a confused mind, but surely even senile dementia took some cognisance, albeit ill-defined, of the environment through which it passed. Mrs Thwaites might not know who had driven her from Parson's Fold to Ember Bay; she could hardly be expected to have noted down the numbers from the registration plates of the vehicle in which she had been carried. But there would be something, surely, some vital if misunderstood impression, that an alert and dedicated detective-sergeant could trace from woolliness to precision. He might even be so vivid in his reconstruction of events that he could persuade the old girl into a rare moment of clarity in which she would tell him all. Sergeant Beamish's view of the immediate future of Sergeant Beamish was a roseate one as the Yorkshire miles swept under his bonnet.

Ember Bay appeared to consist mainly of two uneven stacks of slate roofs that climbed the flanks of an inlet some half a mile across. The resort was served by two roads—one from the south leading in and one from the north leading out. The one from the south, which Beamish was following, was signposted with roadworks, of which the only evidence was a solitary standard of temporary traffic lights, burning arrogantly and long-windedly red. Beamish waited dutifully, the only vehicle in sight, for what must have been five full minutes. He then decided that if the law must be served, the law had to be broken. He drove through the Stop sign and encountered a lorryload of scrap coming over the brow of the hill opposite him. There was an exchange of views in which he came off the worse, being linguistically more of a purist than the lorry-driver. He reversed back to where he had been, the light now having improbably gone to green, only to return abruptly to red (without an intervening amber) for its next five-minute stint before Beamish could let in the clutch. Thus he arrived in Ember Bay in a state of mind that might conveniently be summarized as rattled.

Ember Bay was a former fishing village that had taken unto itself a colony of seaside painters, another of potters, and the minimal amenities of a holiday resort, without expansionist hopes of containing them. Its streets and public places were all lavishly framed in multiple yellow lines and its one-way traffic system was unintelligible to the most intelligent of strangers. Even Sergeant Beamish, brainwashed by a police driving course, was on his way out of Ember Bay by its northern egress before he realized that he had put the operative town centre behind him.

He eventually found the dentist, whose receptionist asked him immediately for the number on his medical card. She was a woman of his own age, distinguished both by her extreme good looks and her bad temper. She looked as if her hell was populated by people who did not know the numbers on their medical cards.

'We spoke on the phone,' he said, 'on the matter of your patient Mrs Thwaites.'

'Mr Hatton cannot see you until after hours.'

'I understand that. I do not need to see Mr Hatton at this stage—in fact perhaps not at all. All I need is the address at which I can contact the patient.'

She scribbled petulantly on the back of an appointment card.

Outside again, he found that his car had not only been boxed in, but also issued with a ticket by a female traffic warden in harridan's black stockings who implied that his warrant card only exacerbated the offence. Somewhere behind the ranks of closed-out-of-season restaurants, shuttered spade-and-pail shops and the empty racks for the deployment of comic postcards, must lie the sea itself, its presence now attested by the lugubrious and frequent but nerve-wrackingly irregular boom of a distant foghorn. The address scrawled by the receptionist needed research.

It turned out to be a house in a Regency terrace on the northern arm of the Bay: a quieter part of the community, this, approachable only up several hundred steps. There was a certain dignity here, a peace interrupted only by a single game of hopscotch on the pavement. The house was occupied by an exuberantly welcoming elderly woman called Mrs Reynolds, who, although a retired nurse, did not usually take convalescents into her home, but sometimes did so to oblige. This she told him as she relieved him of his coat in the hall. She was one of those women who cannot meet a stranger without an autobiographical preamble.

'Your friend is looking forward to seeing you.'

'She is not exactly a friend.'

But Mrs Reynolds had preceded him up the stairs, two treads at a time, with such speed that she missed this. Beamish further classified her as a one-way conversationalist: she was too busy talking to listen.

The house smelled of moth-balls, fire-lighters and

paraffin heaters. As they approached the sickroom, a distinctly hospital smell began to win the day. Mrs Reynolds went straight in, going through the motion of knocking as she opened the door: characteristic number three—she was a woman who liked to observe, however perfunctorily, all the forms.

'Here comes your friend!'

She seemed intent on convincing both sides in advance of the glorious sentimentality of this reunion.

Mrs Thwaites was sitting up in bed in sprightly fashion, her hair ribboned in two bunches that stuck out in absurd fashion at the sides. Beamish thought that he had never seen anyone less suggestive of senile dementia. She beamed on him as he entered, a smile of friendship that must surely have rounded off Mrs Reynolds's day; a smile ruined only by its absolute toothlessness. Her eyes were very much alive indeed—and glad to be so. She said something—quite a long sentence—which emerged only as the lapping of her tongue over vacant gums, further muffled by flabby lips with a tendency to fall inwards. Beamish did not understand a single syllable of her speech, so looking vexed, she repeated the whole statement.

'She says if she'd known how smoothly it was all going to go, she'd have had it done years ago.'

The voice came from the far side of the bed, where the interpreter was seated: an uncomfortable-looking, disgustingly familiar creature, himself the perfect picture of senile decay: Mosley.

And that was impossible. There were no means by which Mosley could possibly have picked up the trail here.

'Show the sergeant your cavity,' Mosley said, and his way with old women was so effective that Nora Thwaites understood him before Beamish did. She opened her mouth moistly and he had to approach, peer down into the red, fleshy depths, and utter admiration for what he saw there.

'Nice, clean job he's made of it, hasn't he?' Mosley said. Beamish agreed and backed away.

'I had the stitches out yesterday,' Mrs Thwaites said

with pride. 'It didn't hurt at all. I'd always thought it was a painful business, having stitches out.'

This time Beamish grasped enough of the sounds she made to put her meaning together along the lines of probability. A conversation with her, on strictly commonplace topics, might not be wholly impossible.

'Now tell Sergeant Beamish the story you told me about Albert Boardman and the root-cutter,' Mosley said.

Mrs Thwaites grinned sheepishly. 'He doesn't want to hear that.'

'He does, you know. He's come a hundred and twenty miles in his motor, just to talk to you—haven't you, Sergeant Beamish? So he doesn't want to miss your best stories.'

But a change seemed to have come over Nora Thwaites. The light of life in her eyes had unaccountably been replaced by a wildness—a mixture of fear, distrust of those about her, and an impotent anger at the impossibility of being understood and believed. 'All I know is, I've been sitting on this hillside for the last six hours, waiting for some conveyance to pass. How'm I going to get back home once the light starts to go?'

She seemed to have turned against Mosley now, and looked imploringly at Beamish. 'Young man—can you get me a conveyance?'

Mrs Reynolds, who had made no sign of being prepared to leave the room, now stepped forward and gave them the benefit of her professional experience. 'She gets mixed up, now and then,' she said.

And Mosley stood up, went to the bedside and looked down at the old woman with a sort of maudlin lovingness. 'Now listen, my dear. I've got to go down into town to attend to some business. Sergeant Beamish has come a long way to talk to you. I want you to be a good girl, and answer him nicely and properly. Tell him everything he wants to know.'

'All I want is a conveyance.'

'Yes, well, when I get back, I'll see what can be done about that. Perhaps the Sergeant himself will take you home in his motor. It all depends on how nice you are to him—how co-operative. You know what co-operative means, don't you?'

And Mosley was out of the bedroom before Beamish could head him off. He was halfway down the stairs before the sergeant had reached the head of the banisters.

'Inspector, where are you going? Hadn't we better make some arrangement about meeting again?'

'I'll be about an hour and a half, I expect,' Mosley said. 'And then I'll come back here. You get what you can out of the old girl in the meanwhile.'

Mrs Reynolds followed the inspector downstairs. Alone on the landing, Beamish looked back at the half-open sickroom door, and for the first time since joining the force, felt a nausea for most things connected with it.

It was two hours before Mosley came back. By then, Mrs Thwaites had mercifully fallen asleep and Beamish was sitting downstairs, listening to Mrs Reynolds, in a fireside chair at the hearth of the old-fashioned, cast iron, black-leaded kitchen range.

Mrs Reynolds was by no means loth to talk, but Beamish doubted whether he had got anything out of her that she would not already have told Mosley. He had learned, for example, how she had come to know Brenda Cryer. But the odd thing was that until Mosley's visit, she had not known that Brenda Cryer was dead. Mrs Reynolds did not take a newspaper or listen to news bulletins; the news, she said, always depressed her.

She knew Brenda Cryer because on Fridays, her shopping day, she always took her morning coffee in the lounge of a small hotel down in the Bay where Brenda had been the receptionist for some years. As often as not it was the receptionist who served the coffee, probably even made it herself behind the scenes; it was that sort of hotel. And Brenda was that sort of receptionist—the woman, in fact, on whom the whole place probably hinged: who had had oversight of chamber-maids, who spotted breakages and failures of gadgets, and had them made good by handymen, who kept an efficient reservation-list, who hired and fired staff, banked the takings, scanned the cook's orders and produced immaculate accounts when the absentee landlord showed periodic interest.

'I don't know how they'll manage without her,' Mrs Reynolds said. 'She needed a change, I suppose. I should have needed one before I'd been there a fortnight. I don't know how they manage to keep the place open. That's why it's so popular with me and my friends for elevenses. There's never a crowd, not even in season.'

'Did she tell you her reason for leaving?'

'Oh, no. It took us all by surprise. And she's going to be missed. If you ask me, she ran the place.'

'You don't know where she used to be before she came here?'

'No idea. She was the pleasantest soul—but she never talked about herself.'

'People didn't try to question her?'

'Why should they? We're not all policemen, you know. She wasn't the sort of person you'd think of asking personal questions.'

'A little forbidding, perhaps? A little toffee-nosed, even?'

'Not on your life. Nothing could be further from the truth. But dignified—though not at all in an off-putting way.'

'Did she ever behave as if there was something in her past that she wanted to hide?'

'Not in the least. Why should she? Sergeant—she's the one who's been murdered, isn't she? You're talking as if some sort of blame attaches to her.'

'I was thinking of her associates. In cases like this, it's very often someone fairly close to the victim who is the culprit.'

'I couldn't say about that.'

'Who were her particular friends in the town, for example?'

I don't know that she had any special ones. The Bay View didn't give her much time. And I never heard her complain about that. She seemed to like work—a lot of it.'

'She had no men friends?'

63

'Not to my knowledge. Of course, there were some who liked to play up to her, especially men travelling away from home. But she knew how to keep them at arm's length without offending them. If someone wanted to flirt, she didn't mind if that kept them at the counter for another round of drinks. She knew how to scotch it if things looked like going too far.'

'Did she never go away for a holiday?'

'Once a year. The hotel generally closed down for three weeks in October. Then she used to go away on her own: an organized tour, as a rule—Majorca, Capri, Crete. Sometimes she stayed in England: the Lake District, the Scottish Highlands. We used to laugh about it—what a change it was for her to stay in someone else's hotel.'

That was the tenor of the conversation with Mrs Reynolds. The retired nurse knew only what she had seen on the surface, and had never seen any reason to doubt —saw, indeed, no reason to doubt now—all that Brenda Cryer had allowed to be known about herself. The friendship between Mrs Reynolds and Brenda had not been deep. Brenda had known that once or twice—to oblige— Mrs Reynolds had taken in uncomplicated patients to nurse in her home, perhaps to give relatives a break. Brenda had written from Parson's Fold to ask if she would take her mother for a week to tide her over à nasty but not uncommon bit of dental surgery. Mrs Reynolds had obliged without expecting anything she could not handle.

'Of course, the old lady's not clear in her mind. But I'm accustomed to that. I had seven years on a geriatric ward. It's only a question of humouring them.'

'And who actually brought her here?'

'It was done through a car-hire firm, with a hired agency nurse.'

'You don't know which car-hire firm, or where they came from?'

'I asked the driver in for a cuppa, but I didn't plaster him with questions. I keep telling you: I don't ask many questions. I took it for granted he was from somewhere near Parson's Fold.'

Whatever he put to Mrs Reynolds, the answer fell

always short of being usefully informative. Beamish was at bottom sufficiently fair-minded to admit to himself that it wasn't Mrs Reynolds's fault. She knew—or thought she knew—only what Brenda had intended her to know.

Beamish was relieved to see Mosley, which was something that he could not previously have forecast. The inspector was in that general state of contentment with society at large which was the only mood in which Beamish had ever seen him. He did not announce how he had spent the last two hours, but there was no sign of excitement to speak of success, nor of despondency to suggest disappointment. They walked down the broad stone steps leading to the heart of the place, and Beamish said he had better ring his wife to let her know how late home he was going to be.

'A good idea,' Mosley said. 'Why not err on the side of accuracy and tell her that you will not be home at all? I propose that we should spend the night in a hotel.'

'*The* hotel?'

'An interesting place,' Mosley said. 'I am curious to see your reaction.'

Bay View was situated in a side-road two right-angles removed from Ember Bay's miniature harbour. Its title's only claim to veracity lay in the fact that there were two small attic windows—of rooms occupied by less favoured members of the domestic staff—from which a glimpse of distant waves might be had when sea-mists permitted.

'I fear that they have no night porter,' Mosley said, 'but they have lent me a key. I fear also that we are too late for an evening meal, for which indeed we would have to have given notice at lunchtime. But I have ordered sandwiches. They do have a bar, which they will open on request, if the barman can be found, which I fear tonight will not be the case. The grille is raised really only for the sale of aperitifs before the meal. The house is only a few days removed from its annual closure, and therefore business has been encouraged to run down. The only other guest beside ourselves is a traveller in trawlermen's cables.'

Mosley inserted the loaned key in the lock and let them in. Only a single pilot light was burning, casting melancholy shadows over the entrance hall and lounge. There was a strong smell of stale beer and the air had been tainted by years of cigarette smoke.

'It seems fair to assume that the house has a merrier air in high season,' Mosley said.

'It seems popular enough with Mrs Reynolds and her friends.'

'For the very fact that it fails to attract the crush of holiday-makers for whom it nominally caters. I am informed that sometimes, during the school holidays, the house is full. But it has become a joke among the staff that no one has ever been known to stay here twice, except hard-bitten commercials, who appreciate a bill made out for twice the amount that they have actually spent. I am also informed that the place was cleaner, tidier and more brilliantly serviced before Mrs Cryer handed in her resignation.'

Mosley switched on a lamp on one of the tables and they saw that sandwiches had indeed been left out for them—the thickest wedges of sandwich that Beamish had ever been offered, though cut so unevenly that they had a curiously tapering effect. The depression made by a large thumb was still visible in one of the rounds, and lace-like fringes of discoloured ham-fat hung over the edges of the crusts. Two glasses had also been provided, together with four small bottles of beer, but no means of opening them. Beamish had an opener attached to his combination pocket-knife, but before he could bring it into action, Mosley—with a degree of dash and sophistication that astounded his sergeant—opened his by bringing it down smartly across a corner of the table.

'Well now: let's have your report, Sergeant. How did you fare with old Mrs Thwaites?'

'Inspector—it's no use. What sort of information do you expect to get from her? Was it just a joke, leaving me like that? She's in an advanced state of mental decay.'

'But with lucid moments.'

'Who the hell can tell where, when and if she's ever being lucid?'

'I admit that it's difficult. I didn't do too well with

her myself. That's why I was anxious for you to try your hand, unhindered by me.'

'An entire waste of time,' Beamish said.

'I challenge that, Sergeant. She's the only evidence we've got of several important aspects of the case.'

'*Evidence*? How can you possibly think of putting a woman like that into a witness-box? Or even of taking a statement from her?'

'I don't mean evidence for the court, lad—or even a document on the file. I mean evidence for your ears and mine: perhaps even the identity of the murderer, no less. Once we know that, our task will be tangibly easier. We shall then know what other, more presentable evidence we'd better be looking for.'

'How can she possibly know the identity of the murderer? She left Jackman's Cottage two days before Brenda was killed. At least I was able to check that date with our dear Mrs Reynolds.'

'True. But she must have had some awareness of the men who came visiting her daughter on previous days. If I'm any judge of character, a much more acute awareness than it would suit her to reveal. She would have seen them, heard their voices, some of the things they said. Perhaps even exchanged a few senile hilarities with them.'

'And got it all mixed up for the rest of her life. She leaps thirty years every few seconds, Inspector. During the time when I was making an honest effort to dig something out of her, she tried to send me once to rescue a sheep that had fallen into a chasm. She mistook me for someone called Bert, with whom she appears to be pursuing a vendetta to the death. And then she thought I was her son, and told me what a bloody fool I'd been to marry a woman from Ribblesdale.'

'Exactly. She is a mine of highly specialized information.'

'And the spine's fallen off the book, and the unnumbered pages have fallen all over the floor. And there isn't an index.'

Mosley chuckled delightedly, in a manner that Beamish saw as yet a new facet of him.

'Very apt, Sergeant. A mixed metaphor, following my reference to a mine—but very vivid. As you say, there are a lot of loose leaves lying about, and we're going to have a testing time, reading them all.'

'Well, for God's sake don't ask me to read them. I made no headway with her at all, and I'm never likely to. And before you tell Superintendent Grimshaw that that's mutiny, do you mind if I submit a written memorandum on the point?'

Mosley looked hurt. 'I'm sure it needn't come to that sort of pass, Sergeant. You and I don't know each other. I don't know where your aptitudes lie. There may be somebody, somewhere who would have a way with someone like Mrs Thwaites.'

'Well, it isn't me.'

'We'll say no more about it, then. There are a few other jobs I'm going to ask you to do.'

Beamish heard this with a marked sense of the ominous.

'A spot of burglary in an hour or so, for example, if you'd care.'

Beamish said nothing.

'And thank you, lad, for looking at her cavity. Very proud of that cavity is Nora Thwaites. I thought it might just have tipped her sympathies in your favour, if you'd said the right thing about her cavity.'

Mosley rolled fat from the crust into his mouth in the most repulsive manner. 'Let's change the subject. What do you think of this place? Are you struck by any anomalies?'

'About its being open to the public at all, do you mean? About its remaining in business?'

'This is not the best time of year to be here, of course. And obviously, it's suffering from the withdrawal of Brenda's touch.'

'The withdrawal of somebody's.'

'Brenda's: the opinion is shared by the town generally. I think we can say that, six weeks ago, Bay View was in better condition than it is now.'

'It could hardly have been in worse.'

'I'll agree that some of the guide-books would be sparing with their stars. So what's that suggest to you?'

'That the British public is always ready to meet a con-man halfway.'

'That wasn't what I had in mind. I was thinking of Brenda's state of affluence.'

'Do we *know* anything about that?'

'We know that she came back to Parson's Fold giving every impression of being well off. A relative judgement, of course, dependent upon the poverty of the observer. But enough to impress her brother, who definitely thought she was well-heeled. She told him she was better off than he is—and he accepted that. And Donald Thwaites may be fighting a losing battle with the hags on his perimeter— but I respect his assessment of economic matters.'

'So—where is this leading us?'

'To two questions. Firstly, the source of her income. Bay View?' Mosley looked over his shoulder at the long shadows in the corners of the shabby lounge. 'Even when a hotel like this is going like a bomb, the bonuses that come the way of the receptionist are not overdone. Tipping by working-class guests during a Yorkshire Wakes Week is finely calculated. This place is owned by a syndicate—faceless out-of-town men who are happy to stay out of town, as long as the dividends keep rolling in. This lot even seems happy enough when they aren't. Since Brenda left, they have put a manager in: a manager, if you ask me, whose job is to preside over its final run-down. There have been managers before, while Brenda was in residence; and she managed them—from behind her reception desk. That is town talk, and I accept it.'

Mosley borrowed Beamish's knife to get into his second bottle of beer.

'And she was here eight years—eight years, remember— those eight years of her we'd lost, when we first started on this. For eight years, she didn't go out much, she can't even have seen a great deal of daylight. She had the sort of annual holiday that can be had by any sensible factory girl who looks after her funds. Eight years! Now why does a thoroughly attractive, pre-eminently capable young woman put up with a dingy existence for eight years? For one of three reasons, I suggest. She may be in love with work for its own sake, using it to kill something, including time. She may have some sentimental sense of loyalty to the institution for its own sake. Or somebody may be making it worth her while.'

'It's only that last that makes sense. But I can't think of any earthly reason why anyone should willingly overpay her for running a place that's perpetually in the red.'

'Then that is something on which we are clearly going to have to concentrate. Eight years!'

Mosley seemed to be taking Brenda Cryer's lot to heart with a deep reserve of human sympathy.

'That's a long time for a woman blessed with free will, who's shown plenty of other evidence in her life of willingness to make up her own mind—and cut off her moorings when she fancies; and who is more than capable, on all the surface evidence we've seen, of making her own way.'

'I don't usually quote poetry,' Beamish said, 'but didn't someone once say something about: *Better to reign in Hell than serve in Heaven?*'

'I don't know: did someone? Eight years!' He seemed obsessed by the prospect. 'I said she had eight years unaccounted for—but don't let's underestimate some of the other gaps. How little we know of her! We know she sweated it out in Rangate from '63 to '65. From about '72 we have her here, the faithful lieutenant of an anonymous out-of-town syndicate. In '65, when she was twenty, she met a man at a works social—and walked out of the world of brake linings. So what was she doing from then till the age of twenty-seven?'

'I suppose that's going to be my next assignment,' Beamish said, his tone not revealing what would be his attitude if it were. The case was beginning to involve him, and although he could not have said when that started to happen, he was now closely listening to Mosley.

'I'm hoping that's going to be one of the things that will, as it were, spew sideways out of the machine. We're going to do a spot of burgling in an hour or so's time, and there's no telling what will come of that. Because there's one more puzzle that I can't see any answer to so far—'

'In my rough notes there are several—' Beamish began, but Mosley went on without seeming to hear him.

'If we accept the reading that Brenda Cryer did reasonably well for herself, what has she done with it all? Where is it? In some deposit account? Invested in the syndicate? In jewellery, real estate, even? Where, even, are her consumer durables? From the few pieces she brought with her to Jackman's Cottage, she'd keen tastes in art and music. So had she no Hi Fi equipment? No prints, books? That's why we're going to feloniously enter her room, presently—the room she had here. I want to find out what, if anything, she left behind; or, to put different terms to the same question—whether she intended to come back when the stint with her mother was finished.'

'You bewilder me,' Beamish said. 'I must say, I thought—' But he did not develop that line, which he saw in mid-stream had got away to a bad start. 'What I'm trying to say, Inspector—you've said an awful lot in the last ten minutes. But doesn't it all start from some pretty confident suppositions?'

'It's got to start somewhere,' Mosley said.

'Yes—but we've got to keep testing the bottom with the plumb-line, haven't we? Now I would have thought a more profitable line would have been her current men friends.'

'I dare say it would. And I'm hoping they'll be spewed out of the other side of the machine.'

Beamish looked at him with interest, not unmingled still with an oblique sense of pity. The old man was not such a fool after all—in his woolly-minded, hit-and-miss, unsystematic, uninformed way. He sat there now, solemnly and eagerly propounding his theories, rather like an old-time insurance man trying to persuade a poor family of the virtues of a cheap industrial policy. Mosley knew a lot about men and women and their motivations—as men and women and their motivations used to be. But had he a clue, for example, of how men and women comported themselves now that the liberating sixties were nearly two decades away?

And then it was uncannily as if Mosley were reading his sergeant's thoughts.

'My mind isn't made up yet,' he said, 'about Brenda's attitude to men. We know she's had at least one unhappy experience with a man, from which she escaped by simply escaping, if you see what I mean. I think there was probably at least one other such soul-searing episode—possibly two. But she hadn't turned her back on men. In a sponge-bag in her bedroom in Jackman's Cottage, she carried an emergency contraceptive kit. I couldn't tell whether it had been used since she had come back to the Fold: I don't think it had. From the encrustation at the mouth of the tube, I'd say it hadn't been used in the last week of her life, at any rate. But that isn't my main point. What struck me was the nature of the method she used: not the system of a woman who was always ready for it: the system of a woman who could quickly make herself ready if need be. Occasional only, in other words. Though whether to oblige a man, who for some reason or other had better be obliged, or whether so as not to miss an opportunity that she fancied herself—that's something I can't at this moment answer.'

'No, Inspector.'

'Well, don't sit there gawping at me. The people back in my foothills may lack the technology for which your Q Division is famous, but we are not without some know-how. Do you know I once retrieved a woman's handbag, containing two pounds, four shillings and six-pence—the whole case turning on a French letter found behind a rabbit-hutch?'

'Amazing,' Beamish said.

'Well, bed, then.'

Mosley got up, assembled the litter of their supper on the tray and carried it over to the apron of the bar-counter outside the grille.

'But I thought you envisaged—'

'Bed noisily, Sergeant. Up again quiet as mice. I'll see you on the landing outside my door, in stockinged feet, at half past midnight.'

The old man headed for the stairs, but turned back on his heel. 'A point I think I ought to make: you were talking earlier on about submitting written memoranda. I'm not fond of that way of looking at things.'

'Please forget that, Inspector—I—'

'No. Let me make myself plain. What we are about to do would undoubtedly be considered illegal in Q Division. In my division, left hands and right hands don't always work off the same circuit. If you wish to be excused from the impending operation, all I ask is that you do not know that it has even taken place.'

'Oh, no—I'm with you, Inspector.'

'You see, I have my reasons for doing it. I could get a warrant for the asking—even at a few minutes' notice at this time of night. But I do not wish it to be known which way my interest is turning. I do not wish that to be known at this stage either in Ember Bay or in the spiritual home of any faceless syndicate. They think I am a doddering old fool and I find that a useful image.'

'Yes, Inspector.'

'Even the Assistant Chief Constable thinks I'm a doddering old fool—and there's no need for you to say, "Yes, Inspector" to that.'

'No, Inspector. But there is one thing I would like to know.'

'Well—if I happen to know myself—'

'How did you find your doddering old way to Ember Bay an hour ahead of me?'

Your doddering old way: Beamish never actually crystallized it out, but it was at that moment that he first knew he was beginning to like Mosley.

'Ah,' Mosley said. 'Friends at court, you see. I happened to think that it would be no bad thing, once in a while, to report progress. There is nothing so confusing as a man who breaks his own lifetime habits. So I rang through to Bradburn when I'd finished at Rangate. And Grimshaw not only told me where you had just left for: he pulled strings at Rangate and had transport laid on for me.'

Beamish suppressed any visible or audible reaction. There were things in this life that just weren't fair.

Ten

_____

At twenty minutes past twelve, Beamish pulled a sweater over his shirt and tucked the bottoms of his trousers into the tops of his socks. At twenty-nine and a half minutes past, he opened his bedroom door. Half a minute later, Mosley opened his.

The corridor was dimly lit by a single dirty, unshaded bulb at the far end. The floorboards, under cold, cracked, brown linoleum, were uneven. Subsidence of the foundations years ago had given a tilt to parts of the house which produced a strange feeling of drunkenness. There was a single, irrationally chosen picture slightly askew on one wall: the Isle of Man—an etching of Peel Castle in the sort of storm in which Wordsworth once saw it.

Mosley knew precisely which way to go, which room had been Brenda Cryer's. Beamish did not ask him how he had come by the information. He was getting used to the marches that the old man stole, his quasi-miraculous efficiency when the present sort of brainstorm was on him. Napoleon, it had been said, preferred lucky marshals. If Mosley had been one of them, there might have been no retreat from Moscow.

They went up a half-flight, on to another short landing where there was no light. Mosley found a switch and pressed it and a bulb fused with a loud click and a blue flash. Mosley uttered a four-letter word followed by a two-letter one, then produced a pencil-torch with whose discreet light he found the door they wanted. About them, the hotel was full of the idle noises of the night: a lavatory with a worn ball-cock washer, the wheezings and knocking of the bizarre patchwork plumbing, a pattering and slithering of mice on linoleum. Beamish did not know what tail-end of staff the hotel still housed, what basic cooks, porters and under-managers might be snoring in cells somewhere in the honeycomb. The rooms on either side of Brenda Cryer's might be occupied; there might not be another soul in this wing.

Mosley had produced some tool from his pocket with which he was attending to the lock. Beamish could not see what it was; probably the old man had an obstinate jealousy of that sort of secret: a basic range of skeleton keys, probably, maybe filched from the kit of some felon years ago. He put his ear down close to the keyhole, listening sensitively for the response of wards and tumblers. The lock did not seem amenable to immediate persuasion.

'Let me have a go.'

Mosley made way for him at once. There was something out of the ordinary somewhere, no obstruction in the mechanism, a smooth motion of tumblers in either direction, but still the door remained locked.

Then footsteps entered the corridor at an angle below them, outside their own bedrooms, the unevenness of gait resulting from something more fundamental than the mere tilt of the floor. Mosley puffed out his cheeks and blew air out slowly through his lips. Beamish looked at him, as if asking for instructions.

'If he comes up here,' Mosley whispered, 'we'll just have to face it out.'

And he was coming up here. A shoulder brushed against a wall, a leather sole missed the edge of a tread, then tired muscles started hauling the man's weight up the half-flight.

'Hullo!'

Friendly enough, anyway—and, apparently, utterly unaffected by coming upon an obvious crime in the commission. Beamish diagnosed the dealer in trawlermen's hawsers, clearly awash with North Yorkshire bitter, clearly capable of little more than finding his way to his own bedroom. But that was evidently a feat which he had often enough achieved against an impediment similar to tonight's.

'Wasting your time there,' the rep said. 'She's gone. Went five or six weeks ago.'

'Oh, aye?' Mosley said, equally friendly.

'Aye. Made a difference to this bloody place.'

'I suppose it has.'

'You'll not find her in there, you know. And even if you did, you'd not stand a chance—not a couple of dead-beats like you two. I mean, she'll let you buy her a gin—and then hide it under the counter while you're not looking.'

He managed to strangle a belch, swallowing with dramatic nausea.

'I don't know why I drink this bloody stuff. I shan't half suffer for it tomorrow. She's not in there, you know. She's been killed.'

'Oh, aye?'

'Aye, it were in t' paper. So you'll get nowt there.'

Beamish was concealing Mosley's skeleton keys in the palm of his hand.

'Well, I'm goin' t' bed. I'm no stopping up half o' t' neight talking to you two silly buggers.'

He turned on his heel and Beamish prepared to catch him as he swayed at the top of the half-flight.

'It's double-locked, anyway,' he said to them over his shoulder. 'T' key has to go round twice. It's t' same wi' all t' staff bedrooms here. That's to protect their bloody virtue.'

He reeled perilously, noisily, but magically protected down the half-flight. Mosley and Beamish heard someone come out of a bedroom a landing below, speak to him. They stood frozen in darkness. Speech was resonant beneath them. The newcomer to the scene was obviously conducting the drunk to his room. Then he too went back where he had come from. The descant of the plumbing prevailed again. The mice, who had taken shelter, returned to their theatre. Beamish gave the tumblers the second pressure that they needed.

And then, after Mosley had quietly closed the door behind them, they found themselves in what was clearly one of the best bedrooms in the house, give or take the taste in interior decoration. It was a corner room, spacious, with a big bow window that commanded a view, if not of the Bay, at least of a roofscape with fanlights and cowls that might delight some kinds of surrealist. Even the decoration was not all that unacceptable, better than was to be found elsewhere in the hotel, reasonably recent, though scuffed by the moving away of furniture, and bearing the inevitable scars and faded rectangles, the cobwebs and chippings of a room that has been cleared.

One of Mosley's bed-rock questions was answered as soon as they were fairly in the room: when Brenda Cryer had moved out of here, she had moved out for good. The bed was stripped down to its interior-sprung mattress. The wall-to-wall carpet was gone, leaving only the rucked-up underfelt. The co-axial cable of a television aerial came in through a window-frame and lay in idle arcs round the skirting-board. Very little of furniture was left: a chest of drawers of a useful size, but that needed work on its veneer, a small writing-table with one of its castors wedged level over a folded cigarette packet. There had been pictures on the wall—more pictures than had eventually appeared in her bedroom at Parson's Fold.

'Well, that's something we now know. When she left here, it wasn't temporarily.'

Mosley went and opened one drawer in the chest after another, even examined the dates of the newspapers with which they were lined, found nothing, apparently, that stirred him.

'So what do we do next?' Beamish asked him. 'Get in touch with the syndicate?'

'They're the last people in the kingdom that we get in touch with. We don't betray any interest in that syndicate until we know a good deal more about them than we do at the moment. We don't approach them from a position of strength: it has to be omnipotence.'

Mosley found a metal wastepaper bin, emptied its contents on to the writing-table and went through them: screwed-up paper tissues bearing cosmetic smears, a cigarette packet of the brand she had been smoking at Jackman's, an empty tube of the sort of contraceptive jelly that she seemed to favour.

'One always lives in hope that they've left something behind that they meant to take with them.'

He brushed the waste back into the bin with the side of his hand, opened one of the drawers in the table, seemed to be having difficulty as it jammed, did not rest until he had pulled it out altogether. Then he reached in with his hand and brought something out. After he had examined it, his features were suffused with seraphic pleasure.

'Something left behind, Sergeant: for instance, the old snap-shot that's fallen behind the back of a drawer.'

It was a colour photograph, amateurishly posed, showing a summer afternoon tea-scene in front of the conservatory of a country house. It was a stone-built house, and from the corner that was visible, seemed to be a sizeable one. Behind it there was a back-cloth of low green hills, a deciduous coppice, an obtuse angle of distant roof. In the middle distance was an end of neatly trimmed box hedge.

An elderly gentleman was sitting at the tea-table, in front of him a china tea-service that one could see, even at this level of photography, to be a family possession of some quality. There were a plate of scones, jam in a server that looked to be of sterling silver and a Dundee cake with one slice cut from it.

The man was in his late seventies at least, exceptionally well preserved and groomed without blemish. He looked kind, happy, above all distinguished—and proud to be in the company that he was keeping.

Brenda Cryer was standing behind him, the only other person in the photograph; though one noticed that the table had been set for three. The picture had probably been taken about ten years ago—she would be about twenty-five, a great contrast to the photographs of her corpse that Mosley and Beamish had seen, with a bloom of maturity in her that was nourished by contentment and security. Her arm was about the gentleman's shoulder—and not as a casual gesture; not blatantly, vulgarly claiming proprietorship, either—but with love; pride, too.

'Well, now, Sergeant—this ought to be a job after your own heart: tomorrow's target. Find out for us where that house is.'

'Oh, yes, that will be right up my street.'

A good deal had happened to Beamish within the last couple of hours. He could not have pictured himself treating Mosley to this ironical banter—except perhaps as safety-valve nastiness for his own relief.

'Where do you reckon that line of hills is? Barrow-in-Furness? Just as obviously the Weald, I'd say. Or do I mean the Wold? No: it's Somerset for certain—'

Mosley was standing by wearing an expression of somewhat idiotic expectancy.

'Of course, it's the stonework that will have the last word. So obviously Yorkshire—or Derbyshire—or Northamptonshire. Or do you think it could possibly be in the Cotswolds? This will be child's play compared with an old woman's wisdom tooth. All I've got to do is get in touch with the estate agents' executive council.'

'You might try the advertisement pages in back-numbers of *Country Life* for 1971 or 1972.'

'We can't know, can we, that it was ever up for sale?'

'Oh, yes, we can. You see, I know it was round about then that this gentleman died. And presumably this property went up for sale. And Brenda Cryer, I wouldn't be surprised, came sadly down in the world. She came here.'

'You are a man for taking mighty leaps, aren't you?'

'I rather regard these as gentle paces. Though I can't be sure of the month of his death. I shall have to look in my journal for that.'

'You are building up the drama very neatly, Inspector Mosley. At what stage are you going to tell me who this gentleman was?'

'Oh, yes, that might be of considerable help to you. He was William—I can't remember his middle name—William Fothergill: of Fothergill, Fothergill, Foster, Sons and Fothergill. He was senior partner for very many years, and it was rumoured that he had a love-nest somewhere— and a young mistress who was somewhat coveted by the few who had been privileged to set eyes on her. Though the story went that she wasn't interested in letting her eyes stray. Maybe they were too firmly fixed on the main chance. Maybe no man had ever treated her quite as old Fothergill did. Incidentally, William Fothergill was the man her father had worked for since the day he'd left school.'

Eleven

'Has something got into Mosley?' the Assistant Chief Constable wanted to know. 'I saw him this morning leaving the office—not actually running, but walking relatively briskly, his chin thrust out like the bow of a snowplough, his chest expanded and his arms swinging as if to a march-step. Oh, and he had a new hat. I could swear he was wearing a new hat. The same shade and style as he has worn since the young Anthony Eden first popularized the model, but I am prepared to stand by my judgement that it was brand new.'

'Very probably, sir. There have been other small symptoms suggesting that Mosley has got his teeth into the Cryer case. I'm sorry that I cannot give you any details. Mosley is always reluctant to produce interim reports that he might be expected to live up to. What impresses me is that Beamish, equally uninformative, seems to be sharing his confidence.'

'Beamish? How is Beamish standing up to this new release of avuncular energy?'

'My fingers are crossed, sir. They seem to be firm friends. I wish I could feel certain that it is going to last.'

'I wish I could share your confidence in Mosley. And how much confidence have you honestly got in Sid Marsters these days?'

'Marsters, sir, is still groping his way through a dark tunnel. He has one of the most unenviable quests that has ever been undertaken by this force.'

'He started it.'

'I know. And he believes in it.'

'And do you?'

'Invariably, sir—for two or three hours after hearing Marsters on the subject.'

'The Chief's been up to London, had an Old Boys' Act session with someone near the top in the DPP's office, showed him the papers in their unfinished state, tried to get a tip or two on the blow of the wind.'

'And?'

'Was told to go for Mason hammer and tongs. The man's obviously a villain, that's what the DPP's right-hand man said. Get him busted. He did also add that if there's the merest haircrack of a loophole in our case, he wouldn't be in our shoes for a fortune. Does Mason suspect that we're on to him?'

'Marsters says he can't possibly.'

'Get Marsters in here at three this afternoon, will you? And drop by yourself.'

It was true that Mosley had bought a new homburg: within a minute or two of the outfitter's opening time. It was also true that he was walking smartly, holding the upper part of his body with military pride. What the Assistant Chief Constable had not noticed, for he had seen Mosley only from behind, was that he was even wearing a new tie, one that combined sobriety with a *soupçon* of *élan*. He rather thought that it was his immediate impact on Fothergill, Fothergill, Foster, Sons and Fothergill that would decide whether he would get a toe of his boot inside a partner's office at all.

He had one contact, and one contact only at Fothergill's: a now elderly maiden clerk who had been trained by Brenda Cryer's father in his own image. Miss Harrison was a thin, dithering woman of limited imagination, fierce loyalty and ferocious discretion, who combined copy-typing with reception, and at the same time acted as ballast to the potential high spirits of certain younger members of the clerical team. She was presiding in her draughty corner when Mosley went in, shortly after buying his new hat.

'I'll tell you what it is, Lilian. I want to have a quiet talk with one of the partners—one of those with his roots in the old days.'

'That doesn't leave many.'

There was in fact only one Foster left of the Sons, and for that reason he was still thought of, at forty-five, by some people as a youngster. No Fothergills remained at all. It was not publicly known how much it cost to buy one's way into the firm; but the probationary period was long, and several were known to have left early.

'I might need to take a little time over it, too,' Mosley said. 'It would be better not to have too many interruptions; and I'd like to get it over in one go.'

'It won't be easy, today of all days.'

But all days were today-of-all-days in Lilian Harrison's crisis-ridden life. She lived on crises as other people are compulsive doodlers.

'There's no one in yet, of course, only Mr Parnell—and he hasn't been with us a year yet.'

'No. He wouldn't do.'

'You'd better come back at a quarter past ten. I'll see what I can do for you after morning conference. Am I allowed to know what it is about?'

'Brenda Cryer.'

'Yes.'

She looked at him without emotion, without even a hint that she saw the mesh of complexities that must lie behind this. Mosley knew very well that Lilian Harrison could tell him more of what he wanted to know than could any of the partners. But he also knew that the only form of interrogation that would have persuaded her to divulge a secret of the firm was not available to the police forces of civilized countries.

He duly reported back to her at ten thirteen and she

permitted herself the ghost of a lip movement, meant to be the hinted smile of success.

'Mr Hartley Mason will see you. He's free now. He can give you half an hour.'

'Which is his office?'

'Mr Jonathan's old one.'

Jonathan Fothergill had died in 1957. Mosley knew the way up the gloomy stairs. Fothergill, Fothergill, Foster, Sons and Fothergill were, as a firm, acutely contemporary-minded, but they cultivated crepuscular gloom and a decor of Dickensian untidiness, their establishment redolent of pink tape, japanned deed-boxes, wax seals and bound statutes. It put the frightener on some clients, gave confidence to others—and also created a deceptive atmosphere of sloth and dawdling-wittedness in which action took place behind the scenes at a sometimes incredible speed. For example, a lot of capital had been multiplied—their own and that of selected clients—in the years of development booms, always legally, but with a smart eye for the critical moment.

Hartley Mason had always been looked on as a slightly enigmatic, slightly controversial acquisition of the Fothergills and Fosters. Hints of uncertainty at top desks had even seeped out into the town. But he had been Mr William's own protégé, brought in about seven years before Mr William died. One of the main reasons for the ripplets of discontent had been Mason's preference for the criminal side, which was something that Fothergills had had little to do with, except on those rare occasions when long-standing clients had found themselves in usually accidental trouble. It was not only that the firm's volume of criminal defence seemed to increase—as did their involvement in legal aid cases—relations with learned counsel developed along well-worn grooves, and a good deal of this sort of business started to come in from far outside the immediate neighbourhood. Hartley Mason put conspicuous energy into cases with which some of the senior partners would rather not have been associated. But Mason's position with the firm, consolidated during the uncertain years by old William himself, had now become unassailable. And Mason did not limit himself to being a link between his clients and their barristers. He had become interested in criminology as a social science—and more particularly in the rights of the depressed classes with whom he had to deal, both before and after conviction. He wrote papers for left-wing reviews on abuse of the Judges' Rules, on procedures after arrest and on the privileges of long-term detainees. No one doubted that Hartley Mason was one of the country's best brains in his preferred specialism, and he rapidly became known as a Prisoner's Friend on a national level—and among professional offenders of broadly-based notoriety. He may not have been popular among his immediate associates, but even they did not slander his professional rectitude. That was left for Chief Inspector Marsters to stir up; but Mosley did not know about that.

He did not greatly care for Hartley Mason. Mason had once dealt with him very snidely in the witness-box (over an affair in which a teenager had been stealing mildly erotic garments from clothes-lines) but both men were too big for this occasion to be remembered when Mosley accepted a leather chair in Mason's office now.

There was a time when the vogue-word for Hartley Mason would have been whizz-kid. In his early twenties, his precocity must have been insufferable to many—though not to a few like William Fothergill who, when he spotted exceptional talent, could be exceptionally tolerant. Hartley Mason was not forty, and had carried with himself to that age not only the reinforced habits of insufferable precocity, but also much of the exuberance of an adolescent well aware of his abilities. Even his rounded features, under his crisp-curled hair, had a youthful, almost puerile appearance—which was belied by the bands of fat under his chin and about his neck. He smiled at Mosley, and Mosley knew better than to assume that this was a propitious signal.

'And what can I do for the Criminal Investigation Department?'

By way of an answer, Mosley simply produced from his wallet the snapshot of Brenda Cryer and William

Fothergill at tea and laid it on Hartley Mason's blotter the right way up for the lawyer to see.

'Ah-ha! I rather thought we might find ourselves up against this.' If Mason was to any extent shaken by what he saw, he concealed it jocularly. 'It has nothing to do with what happened to the poor woman, of course, but I rather thought you might happen upon it in the course of your enquiries. I can see that at first sight, this might appear to complicate your investigation no end—though I can assure you that there is no need for that. I know you will think I am speaking from self-interest. And I cannot pretend that my partners and I will be delighted by the shade of publicity that this is likely to attract. And I hope you do not doubt that I will only too gladly tell you all I can.'

'You were closely in Mr William's confidence over this liaison?'

'I was the only one in the firm who was—though I fancy that one or two of the others had their notions. Old William needed a go-between in the early stages.'

'Then perhaps you can tell from what *milieu* she moved into this country mansion—and in what circumstances she moved out of it into a sleazy hotel in Ember Bay.'

'It was not all that sleazy, Mosley—not in its heyday, when Brenda had the place under her thumb.'

So Hartley Mason was well abreast with the latter part of her life, and was taking no trouble to cover up that fact. He was putting on an image of bold, unembarrassed frankness from the start.

'And it certainly wasn't a country mansion.' Mason looked again at the photograph. 'Though I can see how you come to think so. *I* took this, by the way. Yes: this corner of the wall, the suggested grandeur of the garden: I'm glad for your sake that you didn't have the job of trying to trace the place from this. Actually it's rather a twee little cottage, south east of the Lakes, in a fold that's a sort of *hors d'oeuvre* for the Dales. That's a region that's a bit bleak, you might think, for some people's tastes, but old William had it snug—oh, my God, yes. It was equipped with every work-saver known to the Sunday supplements, and with deep-freezers stocked to withstand a post-nuclear dearth. And as for discretion: the newest office-boy had an idea he was going off somewhere, often for longer than a weekend. But there wasn't a soul who knew the whereabouts of it. By this time, of course, old William had more or less withdrawn from routine work, though he still had the final say in house policy, senior appointments, capital investment, and that sort of thing. However, I'm taking things out of their proper order. It will be far better if I stick to the terms of reference you've so usefully given me. Do smoke, by the way. Please don't feel anything but at your absolute ease.'

Mason took and cut a medium-sized cigar with the rituals of a connoisseur. Mosley preferred a somewhat moistly fuelled little bulldog pipe.

'From what *milieu* did she move to William's love-nest? From the bed-sit quarter of by no means the most salubrious sector of Leeds. I don't know how much homework you've done on her. She'd made a hopeless marriage, let's be frank, while she was still a schoolgirl. And then she'd had a flash of insight: not only the perspicuity to see things as they were, but also the guts to pull out—even at the thirteenth hour. She retreated to a no man's land called Rangate, where wholly admirably—and wholly wrong-headedly—she pursued career-girl plans under cover of squalor and dejection. I'm not sure why. I fancy she felt she had to do some sort of penance. I think she also wanted to teach herself the hard way what it really was like at the bottom. She was a bit of a dreamer, you know, more so in her early years than latterly. Anyway, what's the point of theorizing? That's what she *did*. I don't think she enjoyed what she was doing, but in some perverse way she enjoyed the image of herself doing it. By the way, I know most of this from hearsay. I didn't have more than half a dozen extended conversations with the woman in my life, and the last of those was years ago.'

He paused to flick away a speck of ash from Mosley's pipe, which had somehow strayed on to his blotter.

'Anyway, she got through the self-inflicted sentence,

to all intents and purposes achieved what she set out to achieve. She'd saved up her fees and maintenance and was about to register at a prestigious private secretarial college. I wonder if they'd have taken her? And what she'd have done if they'd contrived some way of showing her the cold shoulder? The question didn't arise, because she never applied. At the crucial moment, she met this man Cryer—I think it was at a works social. And whatever lessons she'd set out to teach herself, she hadn't learned them. Perhaps she wasn't vouchsafed a second flash of insight; or maybe this time it was too much of a bore to pay attention to it. Are some women made to fall into the same trap over and over again? What was it about Brenda that made her fall crazily, scatter-brainedly in love with the sort of man who was the worst sort of medicine for her? Maybe, in the star-spangled stage, it's the attraction of contrasts. Be that as it may, she married Cryer. Bryce had divorced her *in absentia*—she hadn't, of course, defended the suit. They went and lived in Leeds: he was a travelling rep for something highly esoteric and universally unwanted in the machine-tool line. They bought a spec estate semi on mortgage—her savings providing the deposit. And life must have been hell in that corner of Roundhay as they belatedly got to know each other.'

Mason's words sounded strong, but his sense of participation was minimal.

'There were, as they say with such abandoned fairness in the romances, faults on both sides. He turned out to be a compulsive gambler, had no sense of financial responsibility, hadn't even the acumen to make plans, let alone stick to them. When major accounts came in, it was almost a question of drawing out of a hat which one to pay this month. The mortgage repayments were a standing order on a joint account—she'd even been blind enough to fall for that—and the obvious happened. The bank had to stop payments to the building society. She was working—semi-skilled clerical—and then it was the escape from the honeymoon train all over again: the impulse, the brainstorm, the instinct for self-disfigurement, call it what you will. She'd pulled them out of more than one hole, then she suddenly discovered, despite an ultimatum, that he'd run up some other insane debt that he knew they had no hope of clearing. So she threw up her work, said she'd rather be destitute than type invoices eight hours a day, in the company that that entailed keeping, just to grub-stake an idiot.'

Hartley Mason looked cynically across his desk.

'I long ago learned not to lose sleep over trying to analyse human motivations. I don't know what makes men and women do the things that they do. Enough for me that they bring me an income by doing them. Maybe she hoped that a really cold douche might persuade him; it certainly persuaded her. After a few days' first-hand acquaintance with destitution, she left him: hence the bed-sit. A new job, an attempt at incognito, a new loss of identity. And this time she was the one who started exploring divorce. She made an appointment with a city solicitor, was in the waiting-room when old William came out of the inner office; he'd been paying a personal call about some top-level urban development. Of course she recognized him—she was the daughter of his own managing clerk, remember—and something about the way she was looking at him made him look twice at her. Then he, too, remembered. It was some years, you'll understand, since he had seen her.

'"Don't I know you?" and the usual sequences. And he was struck.'

Hartley Mason embarked on a new phase, a sense of involvement that might or might not have been sincere. 'I dare say you knew William Fothergill.'

And Mosley had; not, naturally enough, from the same angle or at the same depth as Hartley Mason had— but enough, rightly or wrongly, to have been impressed by him.

'He was a remarkable man. I'd go so far as to say a wonderful man. It goes without saying that I am prejudiced: he was my sponsor in Bradburn, and I don't know where I might have fetched up—or foundered—without him. But people who did not know him intimately did not know how sensitive he was—or what uncomplaining suffering he had gone through: he had been a widower for fifteen years. And he was struck by Brenda at first sight—I mean, of course, at first adult sight. And let's be frank: she was a striking woman. This photograph here says it all; or most of it, anyway. She'd still not pulled out of the bad times, that day William met her in Leeds. That was in her face, and there was something about it that gave her added depth and appeal. Old William was struck; and he took her out to dinner that evening.'

Mosley sat back in his chair as if the rest hardly needed telling.

'He had me do a little discreet checking up on her, which is how I come to know as much about her as I do. I know that sounds a bit mean, a bit mercenary, perhaps: which is one good reason why he farmed it out, instead of doing it himself. And then he propositioned her: not as a potential mistress, though there was a strong understanding that that was the way it might go, if it suited both sides. She was to be his housekeeper-companion, in a secluded retreat he had acquired not all that long ago. He was a contemplative man, he was courteous, he was tired—and he had been lonely for a very long time.'

Mason sounded more deeply involved with William Fothergill than he did with Brenda.

'I must give Brenda credit for a good deal of uncertainty at first, though, for all practical intents, she was on to a good thing. William wasn't likely to last more than another ten years at the most; she'd still be a presentable woman when her responsibilities to him were done. She'd lost her taste for suburban domesticity—and she found William sympathetic, fascinating company—a man who knew how to treat a woman. The projected settlement was not only handsome, it could not have been drawn up by more reliable hands. Sex wasn't an overriding consideration. If it happened, it happened—and let's hope it did, for both their sakes; I can't tell you whether or not. I did some of the negotiating behind the scenes. William leaned over backwards to avoid overbearing persuasion, but I knew what he went through while she was making up her mind. I must say it was a relief to me when she agreed to a trial month on a strictly housekeeper basis. You must take my word for it: it went on from there to become the sort of idyll that they both deserved. Old William adored her. She had never been treated properly. Only two things spoiled it.'

Mason looked at Mosley as if challenging him to say what they were; but he avoided such parlour-games.

'There came a day when William hadn't been back to Bradburn for nearly a month. There were documents that required his personal signature—a re-investment of maturing bonds. There were rumours about what sort of private life he was leading—some of them not very kind, but you'd be surprised how many people near to him took pleasure on his behalf. No one knew who the woman was. Only two people in the office knew the whereabouts of his hide-out. I was one of them, but this wasn't generally known, because William thought it best to keep dark the part I'd played in the affair. The other was Brenda's father, who had the address under lock and key, and could use it in emergency on authorization from one of us. No man could have been a safer depository, and it was he who took the papers for signature—because I was nailed down by a long court hearing. I thought it utterly safe to send him, because he was the last man on earth to bruit it abroad that it was his daughter who was involved. That was how I saw it: I did not know that he would take it the way that he did. There were quirks in his character that I did not know—and that I probably would not have understood if I had. The discovery that Brenda was his master's mistress was more than he could support. Loyalty to the one and the disgrace of the other were a conflict he could not resolve. I suppose most men would have come to terms with it in time: but not Arthur Thwaites. He had been brought up in a narrow school. His life's comfort had been a simplistic morality. His attitude to servant-master relationships was virtally feudal. He had been suffering from high blood pressure for some years, and he had a stroke when he got home from that trip. It was a hideous business.'

'I can imagine. Did—?'

91

'Did what, Inspector?'

'Did Brenda's mother ever get to know what he had discovered, up in the Dales?'

'I don't know, Inspector. There were things that it was no part of my life to go into. And there was worse to follow—for Brenda. The liaison in that little cottage lasted about seven years. When William Fothergill died— mercifully it was not at the cottage, it was on one of his infrequent cross-country trips—she sat it out in solitude for a couple of months, waiting to hear news from us. It fell to my ultimate lot to take it to her: that despite promises and assurances, there had been no ultimate settlement drawn up by old William—and certainly no trace of anything on our files. Yet this was something he had insisted on handling himself: he would not even trust it to me. It defeats me still, as it defeated me then. It cannot possibly have been insincerity. He was far too experienced a man to have left ends loose. He was not the one, certainly, to hesitate to think about his own demise. He left Brenda high, dry and penniless—without title even to the articles of furniture about her, which had undeniably been gifts. I was devastated—the more so because the tidying-up of all this—if that's what you can call it—somewhat naturally devolved on me. There was nothing—but nothing—that I could do for her. Her only hope was from his own son and daughter—who had never even formally met her—and they saw no reason why they should make any gesture.'

'She must have been flattened.'

'Indeed, I began to despair for her. This was her third devastating experience of men. But, being Brenda, her spirit revived. That was where Bay View at Ember Bay came in. It was a vacancy she had seen in the press. I knew about it, because she asked me to act as reference. It was a post for which she had no qualifications—and yet every qualification. She had common sense, energy, taste. She could type and keep books, get the best out of people. And by the grace of God, that was the way the syndicate saw her when they interviewed her. I might say that few candidates for any job were backed by the sort of reference that I wrote for her behind the scenes.'

'So why did she leave Bay View?'

'I don't know. I didn't stay in touch. I looked in on her just once, when I had my own family up in Scarborough —and the hotel was going like a bomb. She was busy eighteen hours of a summer day—and loving it. Well, sir: I've omitted a lot. Damn it, I've *forgotten* a lot—but there you have the bones of the story. I dare say you're bursting with questions—but just at the moment—'

He looked at his watch. Mosley stood up. The internal phone on Mason's desk gave the sketchiest tinkle, as if it was a matter of sheer luck that the hammer had contacted at all: Lilian Harrison, letting him know that his next appointment had arrived.

'He can come up at once.'

Mason smiled at Mosley: an indication that he had said all he was going to say about Brenda Cryer, that his interest in her was over. Mosley moved to the door, opened it. Mason had made no move to show him out of the room. On the landing were bare wooden tables, loaded with papers roughly tied up in manila folders. Most of them must already have been there when Mosley first joined the force.

Heavy feet started to climb the stairs: the next man, with the next problem—something perhaps that was going to affect the pattern of his life, cost him maybe half his savings or more.

The newcomer turned and went back down the three treads he had already climbed, to let Mosley come down. In the gloomy recess at the bottom, Mosley felt strong fingers clasping his arm—and an angry whisper: 'What the blazes are you doing here?'

It was Chief Inspector Marsters, florid, blustering and anxious.

'Duty call,' Mosley said, like a password.

'Who've you been to see?'

'Hartley Mason.'

'And what case are you on that needs take you to him?'

'Brenda Cryer.'

Then Lilian Harrison was speaking from her draughty desk, so placed that it commanded several corners. 'Mr Mason *is* free, Chief Inspector.'

Twelve

Chief Inspector Marsters was trying to say something—something that came up against an impediment in his speech from which he did not usually suffer. Eventually he managed to produce it. 'Mosley!'

There were three of them in the Assistant Chief Constable's office. The ACC himself was like a man in an earthquaked building who is waiting with crossed fingers to see how much of it is going to fall on him. Detective-Superintendent Grimshaw, by nature and empirical persuasion a conciliatory man, was doing his best to hold himself in reserve, knowing that Marsters would take any premature attempt to placate him as an insult.

'Mosley! For eight months now I have been waiting in the shadows, flicking a fly across the waters over Hartley Mason's head. I have moved from covert to covert, never rustling a grass. Last night I sat at my desk from the smaller into the larger hours and orchestrated the final approach down to a development for every variation.'

Did the man think he was fishing, or composing a bloody symphony?

'I had worked out the optimum order in which to play my hand. I knew just what I was going to keep to myself, just how I was going to throw him the crumbs, just how one little thing was going to lead to a slightly bigger one until the trap was sprung. You've got to understand,

Tom—one detail out of place, and Mason was alerted. And Mason alerted meant Mason lost. In that half hour, Mosley had not merely alerted Mason: he had taken him on a conducted tour of half the points I was building up to make—without, I may say, understanding the implications of a single one of them. Not only had Mosley warned him off—he had constructively rehearsed him through his defence against every finely balanced point that I was about to make. It was as if a trout had suddenly stuck its head out of the water and asked for a Greenwell's Glory instead of a Gold Butcher. Hartley Mason sat there openly preening himself on the luck of the gods. "May I refer you, Chief Inspector, to a statement I made less than ten minutes ago to a colleague who appears to be several stages ahead of you?"'

The Assistant Chief Constable sat wishing that Marsters would have a stroke and be done with it. There would be an untidy few minutes while they carried him from the carpet to the mortuary; but at least a period of calm would follow.

'Oh, I don't know,' Grimshaw said smoothly. 'We have to remember that this *is* Mosley's first murder. And you have to take your hat off to him: he has moved.'

'He has blundered!' Marsters said.

'Be fair, Sid. Most of the time with Mason you were talking about completely different matters. You'd guessed there had to be a woman in it somewhere, acting as go-between. I'll give you your due—you even thought it might have been old William Fothergill's fancy-piece. But it took Mosley to tell us who she was.'

The veins in Marsters's temples looked dangerously close to final rupture.

'You knew there had to be a report centre somewhere —a safe house. It took Mosley to go toddling across Yorkshire in a straight line to Bay View.'

'And he doesn't know why!'

Marsters was saved from apoplexy by suddenly going the other way; he came near to tears.

'He knows who she was, but he doesn't know what

she was doing. He knows where she was, and he doesn't know why.'

The Assistant Chief Constable looked from one face to the other, wishing that Grimshaw would wave a magic wand.

'We could, of course, always tell him,' Grimshaw said mildly.

And that did it. Marsters overcame the temptation to weep. 'Splendid! So why not take the affair entirely out of my hands and make the whole issue over to Mosley? Why not give him a direct line to the Director of Public Prosecutions? Why not absolve him completely from having to make any reports to us? We shan't lose any sleep over what we don't know about, shall we? And as for me, what better use could you find for me than prowling round hen-houses and warning kids who pinch sweets from Woolworth's?'

The Assistant Chief Constable closed his eyes and appeared to be devoted to silent prayer.

'I've been looking over your crime reports, Jack,' Grimshaw said, 'and murder is all very well. It makes a change for us all, once in a while. But we mustn't neglect our main reason for existence, must we?'

Mosley, in the one chair in Grimshaw's office in which he never felt at ease, looked at his superior with a face that could not be said to bear any expression whatever.

'What I am getting at, Jack, is that your bailiwick doesn't seem quite to have that untroubled air we have come to associate with it. Don't think I am being critical. But to a mere reader of morning reports, there are things going on up in your cloughs and dales that would not have been going on a fortnight ago. Unsolved crimes: a whole crate of tangerine oranges spirited away from a pavement display in Lower Spritwell. The word HOAR—spelt as if it referred to an overnight frost—printed in weed-killer on a council-house lawn on the Bracegirdle Estate. And geese, Jack: twenty-five of them, vanished as if some Pied Piper had led them overnight into a hole in the flank of

Lanthorn Hill. Can it possibly be true, we have asked ourselves in this office, that a whole flock of bloody geese has been driven from the very nerve-centre of Jack Mosley's patch?'

'I expect someone is thinking ahead to the Christmas trade,' Mosley said. 'As a matter of fact, I was on my way up there when you sent for me.'

'That's what I hoped I would hear: first things first. The Chief sets great store, you know, by some of the less showy aspects of our commission. That is why he has decided, in his wisdom, that he would like you to concentrate on all the bits and pieces that are outstanding in your area. Try and produce a clean sheet in the next forty-eight hours.'

He waited for Mosley to ask the question; but Mosley could treat his superiors exactly as he treated his suspects. He remained silent.

'He has asked me to take general oversight of the Brenda Cryer affair, and Chief Inspector Marsters will be looking after an important lateral issue. We feel that this will relieve you of anything that might interfere with your own work.'

Mosley gave Grimshaw the full effect of his round, baby eyes.

Grimshaw looked away. 'You will understand, of course, that Marsters and I have to steer our way through some dangerous shoal waters. There are certain things, with which I need not trouble you, that are very delicately poised. It would be only too easy, with the best will in the world, for an unintentional fringe-movement to upset that poise. I hope I am not talking in riddles, Jack. There are times when a police force, like an intelligence service, must work on the need-to-know principle. Therefore I must ask you, if you do happen across anything that you think might have a bearing on the Cryer case, to do nothing about it—nothing at all except to inform me. You know you can always get me on a direct line.'

Mosley did not even nod.

'There is just one other thing, Jack—and I am sure it will come as another great relief to you. It will no longer be necessary for you to carry the additional burden of Sergeant Beamish. An excellent man in his own way, of course, but apt to become bored and restless over weed-killers and tangerine oranges. So we shall be retaining Beamish to help us.'

Mosley went straight not to Lanthorn Hill, but to Piper's Fold, to Mumper's Farm, whose tenant, 'young' Neddy Sladburn, he had made several unsuccessful attempts to contact over the last few days.

Mumper's was another example of the failed intake: a squat little stronghold of farmhouse, scarcely bigger than the average labourer's cottage, that had sheltered various unrelated generations who had starved slowly on the proceeds of the half-reclaimed moors above. Neddy Sladburn —known as 'young' at forty by everyone in the Fold—was not starving. It was true that he farmed: he had fifty sheep at large on the hills. He had a dozen hens, one cow and a sheepdog. His income came from his other occupation— definitely considered youthful by the people of Parson's— as a breaker of old cars. There were always a dozen or so of them littering his yard, much to the anger of the District Council, who had been refusing him planning permission to operate his trade for years, prosecuting him, giving him notice and final notice, harassing him with clerks, solici-tors' letters and bailiffs. Neddy, for his part, had produced appeals, counter-appeals, committees of enquiry, last-minute stays of execution and ambiguous rulings by the Ombudsman: a perpetual state of running warfare in which the one feature that remained constant was the assortment of double-decker buses, old baker's vans, Ford Prefects and rusting old station-wagons that were visible on his hillside for a radius of many miles. The odd thing about Neddy was that he appeared to make his living without any visible diminution of his stock-in-trade: he never seemed to part with an old vehicle. What he did was to study, with a phenomenal memory and a genius for economic forecasting, the desperate pleas that appeared in the smaller advertisements of the trade press. Neddy Sladburn asked—

and apparently got—astronomical prices for such unconsidered trifles as a handful of obsolescent screws, an out-of-date coach-bolt, a superseded radiator-cap, a discontinued line in exhaust manifolds, or a still serviceable gasket for an engine of which the wide world contained only one other working example. But it was not for mechanical succour that Mosley now called on him: Neddy Sladburn had also been Brenda Cryer's—then Brenda Thwaites's—boyfriend, in the far-off schooldays before Charles Bryce had accelerated into her life in a red sports car.

'I've been wondering when you'd be coming.'

Neddy Sladburn withdrew himself from under a chassis from which he was retrieving cross-members that might have been made of platinum for the price he was proposing to ask for them.

'Well—actually—'

'Come in the house. Have a cup of tea.'

Neddy Sladburn ran a bachelor establishment. The sentimentalists of Parson's Fold liked to believe that at nineteen he had been so aggrieved by Brenda's treachery that he had vowed never to take up with another woman. He took Mosley now into a house that had certainly not had the benefit of a woman's hand during Neddy's twenty years' tenure of it. He was a man whose demands upon his environment were as little as his expenditure on it. He took things as he found them—and let them remain so. And Mosley was quite unaffected by the sugar-sack curtains, the tray of drained sump-oil that for some obscure reason had been brought indoors, the stained brown enamel mug out of which he was presently happy to drink his tea.

'Aye; it were a bad business. And if I can help you lay hands on the bugger that did it—'

'I was hoping you'd feel like that about it,' Mosley said.

'You can say what you like about her. She never harmed a soul in the world bar herself.'

'I was thinking about geese,' Mosley said.

'Geese? What geese?'

'Lanthorn Hill. Last Thursday night. Jimmy Pendlebury's.'

'Lanthorn Hill? That's fifteen miles away. I've not set foot up Lanthorn Hill for ten years—not set eyes on Jimmy Pendlebury for longer than that. How could I tell you anything about geese on Lanthorn Hill? I was thinking you'd come to see me about Brenda Cryer.'

'Geese,' Mosley said, obsessively, but without emphasis. 'I've been taken off Brenda.'

Neddy considered this piece of intelligence with perplexity verging on alarm. 'Who's on the Brenda business, then?'

'Tom Grimshaw.'

'That daft bugger? I don't mind telling you, Mr Mosley, anything you want to know. In fact I've been waiting my chance. But Tom Grimshaw will have to whistle for answers.'

'Marsters is with him,' Mosley added casually, as if to secure the point.

For a few seconds, Sladburn hid his face in his capacious and oily hands. 'Well, I suppose somebody thinks he knows what he's doing. And I dare say you'll pull it out of the bag for them in the end, same as you have done before. I don't think, looking back, that it would have worked out all that well, me and Brenda; but I was very fond of her. Very fond.'

He allowed himself a moment of sentiment, gazing unseeing at his meal-table, on which the remains of his breakfast occupied such space as was not taken up by an old-type magneto he was stripping.

'I don't suppose it would have worked out. One of us would have had to change, and what I know of her, it wouldn't have been Brenda. I was a couple of years older than her, you know, and we'd always used to travel together on the bus, while I was still at school. And then, after I left, if there was ever anything on in the village—a dance, or one of the old vicar's barbecues—the pair of us would go together. Sometimes, of a Saturday or Sunday, we'd go for a walk; over the Beacon, or else across into the Trough. Her parents didn't reckon me, of course, which made Brenda keener than ever to come out with me. She was like that, even as a kid. And we used to have the most God-awful rows. I mean, it was one long slanging-match. I don't think we ever agreed with each other on a single mortal thing. That was the joy of it: we could say any mortal thing to each other—and did!—and still be together at the end of the day, and fixing up a trip to the pictures, down at Bradburn, next Saturday. It was relaxing, that's what I'm trying to tell you. We knew each other inside out, that's the truth of it—and we weren't afraid of telling each other. "Why don't you clean yourself up, Neddy," she'd say. "You really are bloody disgusting. Look at your fingernails. I don't know why I allow people to see me out with you." And I'd say, "You're not the only one who's taking chances that way, you toffee-nosed bitch. I've barely a friend left in Parson's Fold since I started walking out with thee. They all think I'm trying to get into t' New Year Honours List or summat." Aye; happy days, Mr Mosley! Then she had to take up with that fellow from Goosnargh, cracked on he was an artist. Just because he had that two-seater, that's what I thought it was at first. And when I heard they were getting wed, I thought at first my mind would shear a cotter-pin.'

He looked at Mosley for a moment of simple and uncontrived confession.

'I allowed myself the luxury of feeling hurt, Mr Mosley.'

A cat climbed on to the table and began to lick his breakfast plate. He did not interfere with it.

'And I don't know how long it took me to realize that of course there couldn't have been anything in it for Brenda and me. For one thing, I know I'm a dirty bugger, and that's only the beginning of it. All the same, when she came back here, when she brought her mother home from that place where that half-baked bloody paint-merchant and his wife had sent her, I thought to myself, well, I'll go down and see her. And that wasn't because I'd any thought of taking up from the old days.'

Neddy laughed; not a very convincing effort to show unconcern for himself and his life.

'Just because we'd been old friends, and I thought she'd still be good for a laugh: and perhaps another bloody good row. Well: I did go down there. I went there several times, if the truth is told—but I only saw her the once. Because every other time I went, she had somebody with her; I'm not beyond a bit of window-corner peeping you know, or listening. And once it was her brother and his wife. And my God, were those three having a barney! Hammer and tongs it was, and I tried to make out what it was about—I always did have the reputation of being the nosiest Parker in the Fold—but some voices carried better than others and I never really got hold of the thread of it. But it was her brother who'd somehow or other got her goat. And this wasn't comic stuff, like the pair of us used to come out with, up in the hills. This was hate, Mr Mosley. This was the sort of hate that gets into some people's lives—and then they end up on hearth-rugs with bullets through the back of the neck. It was something he'd done, and I don't know what. Or, rather—it was something he hadn't done; something he ought to have told her and hadn't. "I'm not blaming my father at all," she said. "He just couldn't help it. He never did me a scrap of good in his life, so I wouldn't expect him to spoil his record on his death-bed. What he did was all he knew how to do. There are some people, and you'd be among them, I suppose, who'd say it was all I deserved. But you could have told me. If only you'd told me!" And Donald Thwaites said something I didn't catch—something soft and self-satisfied, like the man is. And that got her worse on the raw. "Don't you go making excuses like that," she said. "Where do you think this is that we live? The middle of the flaming Sahara?"'

Neddy Sladburn had regenerated a good deal of emotion in the telling of this. There were red spots burning over his cheekbones.

'Well, other times I went, and she had visitors. And I don't know who they were: different men. Well: that was her affair, wasn't it? But this particular evening, I'd left it fairly late on, thinking that would give her the chance to bed her mother down, and there's a car standing out in the lane. So I'm round to my usual corner of window. And there's a voice that I recognize, though it took me a long time to place it. It was only when he moved so I caught sight of his face that I knew who it was. Three guesses, Mr Mosley?'

'I'm only supposed to be here about geese,' Mosley said.

'Bugger you and your bloody geese! I'll tell you who it was. It was Hartley Mason: that smooth operator that joined Fothergills ten years ago. I knew him, because the police put him up to prosecute me a couple of years back. They always point a solicitor at me, knowing my habit of speaking up for myself. And he threw the book at me: tread gone on two tyres, no windscreen washer fluid, faulty contact on tail-lamp, no MOT certificate and a jagged edge on the bumper that they reckoned was a danger to other road-users. It was a car I'd just bought; I was driving it home. Anyway; beside the point. Why I'm telling you this is that Hartley Mason and Brenda were having a worse row than I'd heard with her brother, perhaps not as rowdy, but dead icy. Danger-signals; and again that feeling came to me—Brenda was into something that was out of my class: not just a family quarrel. And not a woman breaking it off with a man. This was something nasty, Mr Mosley. "I want out," she said. "And when I say I want out—I'm out." Good old Brenda! That's the way she always talked—and did things. And I think Mason knew it too, because after a bit, he stopped trying to persuade her. "Well, you disappoint me," he said. "And if ever you change your mind, you know there's always a niche for you." And she said, "Yes, well, I might always take you up on that, but somehow I don't think I will. But if it's a favour you're wanting to do me, I'd like you to set Matty Pearson on to something for me—something right up his street." Who's Matty Pearson, Mr Mosley?'

'Oh, an enquiry agent. The Fothergills have kept him in business for years. This is all very interesting, Neddy—but it isn't taking us any nearer our feathered friends.'

'Oh, to hell, Mr Mosley. Will you stop talking about

those blasted geese? I haven't finished what I'm telling you. Do you want to hear it or don't you?'

'Seems to me I just can't help hearing it.'

'Well, I did go back to see her. And it wasn't at all like I'd expected. I won't say we were right back where we'd started, because that wouldn't be true. And in any case, we'd both learned too many lessons since those days. But we were glad to be with each other, if you see what I mean. We weren't putting the clock back—but we were looking back at an old clock—together. And I saw she was looking away from me. And I thought, hell fire, can't she stand the bloody sight of me?—I'd cleaned myself up no end, Mr Mosley. And then I spotted it. She had tears in her eyes, and didn't want me to cotton on. We talked about everything under the sun, and odd things that had happened where there wasn't much sunshine. And we didn't have a row. God, that's just come to me! We didn't have a row! But she said to me suddenly, "Do you still love me, Neddy?" And it wasn't a question that meant what it said—because we both knew by now what love is and what love isn't. But it was meant to be leading somewhere, so I let it lead. "Well, will you do something for me, Neddy? Will you turn your hand to a little burglary for me?" And I said, "Now look, I don't know how you think I've spent all these years out of your control—" Hell fire, Mr Mosley, you don't think *I* nicked those bloody geese, do you?'

'I know very well you didn't, Neddy.'

'Small mercies, then. So I said to her, "I might now and then have overdone the profit margin on a pair of car-door sills. But burglary—no. I've always regarded that as a bit on the specialized side." And she said, "I don't think this is a case that calls for very great skill, Neddy. In fact, I've thought of several little ways in which it can be made very easy for you. As they say in the trade, I would set it up for you. I think there might not even be much in it. It's information I'm after, not loot: even negative information." And what she meant by that, I don't know. I was too busy thinking to myself, does she want me to break into Fothergills? Because that's where Edward Sladburn,

105

Esquire, Mister, draws his line. Even for Brenda. Then she said, "I want you to insinuate yourself—" that's the word she used, Mr Mosley—"I want you to insinuate yourself into the Old Rectory." But what I was supposed to go there and look for I never did find out, because that's the moment for another car to draw up outside. And she let Hartley Mason in. So I just said to her, in a loud voice, like, "You obviously need a new clutch. I think I know where I can put my hands on one for you." And I'm off into the night.'

'Yes, Neddy.'

'Well, doesn't all that interest you, Mr Mosley?'

'Not as much as certain of God's creatures that I don't know whether I dare mention again.'

'You want me to go slogging up Lanthorn Hill, to find out who swiped Jimmy Pendlebury's geese? Doing your job for you, and not for the first time?'

'No, Neddy. I don't think there's much point in going up Lanthorn Hill. Jimmy's geese were the only things up there worth stealing, and they've gone. I want you to do a bit of strategic planning for me. Just imagine you're the mastermind behind an outfit that's on to a good thing: getting poultry direct from the producer to an uninquisitive wholesaler. You're working this district. Where are you going to strike next?'

'Ah!'

'I hope the problem interests you, Neddy.'

'In the abstract, Mr Mosley. That's another word I learned from Brenda—twenty years ago. But what about all those other things I've told you about her?'

'Oh, I dare say I might pass them on to Tom Grimshaw—if I come across him.'

Thirteen

Mosley did not often start his working day in the central office, unless he had been sent for—and not always even then. It was something more than a headquarters, a hub of communications, intelligence and executive resources; there was primeval humanity at work here, as well as the autonomic nervous system of the force. It was a world of latrine rumours, of whispers behind cupped hands, of esoteric references to the high and mighty in trouble. Mosley had been known to go for a fortnight without ever setting foot in the place.

The sight of him therefore at twenty minutes to nine, making an unparalleled series of telephone calls, ticking off items on what looked suspiciously like an ergonomic progress chart, and referring constantly to the Ordnance Survey map, was one which aroused anxious curiosity in several already troubled hearts. To Marsters and Grimshaw, doing their best to creep in without his seeing them, the sight of Mosley operating as advanced an instrument of technology as a telephone was in itself cause for concern. Mosley undoubtedly controlled one of the most fruitful bucolic spy-systems in the history of detection, but it was rumoured that contact was mostly by smoke-signal.

Grimshaw could therefore not resist the temptation to pass down by Mosley's desk and extract heavy humour from his basic fears. 'I'd been hoping to see you with goose-down in your hair by now, Jack.'

Mosley looked up at him with eyes slightly bloodshot. 'Golden egg coming up,' he said, gathered up his papers into the old wartime respirator bag that was his executive briefcase and left without extending further courtesies.

Things had begun to move the previous evening, when he had received a visit at his home from Neddy Sladburn, driving a pick-up truck that looked as if it had been put together from remnants of his stock-in-trade which he could not have offered to the most specialized of buffs.

'Been doing a day's unpaid work on your goose-rustlers,' Neddy said. 'And I don't like the look of it. Foreigners.'

'Foreigners?'

'Well—visitors.'

'How far afield?'

'Sheffield.'

'Bad,' Mosley agreed. 'How did you get on to them?'

'They'd been up Lanthorn Hill that same morning: Cortina Estate, G registration, Sheffield Post Office stamp on the licence. Made out they had a radiator leak and went to Jim Pendlebury's for a can of water. That's when they must have cased the joint.'

'Aye.'

'And there's another thing—about Brenda—'

'Oh, aye?'

'It didn't come back to me yesterday until after you'd gone. You remember she'd asked Hartley Mason to do her a favour? She said she wanted a job doing by a man called Matty Pearson—'

'Matty Pearson, that's right.'

Neddy Sladburn's eyes narrowed.

'You look as if you know him.'

'We've come across each other in our time.'

'And aren't all that fond of each other, I dare say?'

'Oh—Matty can be handled.'

'Well, she wanted him set on to her brother, that's

what I've remembered. *Set on* to him. Those were the words that she used.'

Mosley left the office, with Grimshaw still looking down at the space he had vacated at his desk. He made his leisurely way round to the Bracegirdle Estate and stood and contemplated a pocket handkerchief of lawn where a moral libel—or, at least, a moral statement—had been etched by a moving finger writing in weed-killer. It took him an hour to clear up the matter. Number 37 was occupied by a young married woman with two children who called her *Mummy*, but who said *Daddy* over the fence to the man who had moved in next door, in replacement for a man who had moved up two Avenues and a Close to live with a woman called Deirdre, whose husband had gone across the road to cohabit with Sandra, whose man had turned out to be a homosexual and was now shacked up with an Italian waiter on the far side of Bradburn. It was a simple matter of mental arithmetic to see that this chain-reaction had left one woman unrequited. Her name was Kim, she had four children and a diabetic mother-in-law, and she it was whose moving finger had writ. Mosley assumed that she would be bound over to keep the peace.

He spotted a milk-tanker on its way back to a distribution centre at the foot of one of the dales and organized himself a lift to Lower Spritwell, where he applied himself to the loss of a tray of oranges. This gave him a great deal of trouble: the most exhaustive cross-elimination of movements in the village street proved stubbornly unproductive. A short chat with the headmistress of the village school drew forth only an unfeigned faith in the innocence of her flock; and, once intuitively impressed, Mosley was not given to labouring an approach. It began to look sadly like an inside job, always, in Mosley's experience, the most melancholy of unfoldings. And he was at a loss to see any motive for it in the present case. Why should Peter Morridge, a shopkeeper of the old breed, either steal from himself or falsely pretend that he had been robbed? Or why should his female assistant—no fly-by-night, a widow in her depressed mid-sixties—soil her fingers with a deed that must surely have left her with a well-nigh impossible problem of disposal?

Mosley postponed further consideration of citrus fruits until after his lunch, a pork pie consumed from the palm of his hand in a discreet corner of the churchyard. He then paid a visit to the telephone kiosk, for which he appeared to have furnished himself in advance, to judge from the large supply of coins which he marshalled beside the slots before consulting his list of numbers. He made precisely the same number of calls as he had made earlier from the office, and, indeed, to precisely the same acquaintances—who included four rural constables, one vicar, two licensed victuallers and an old lady who lived alone. One reply was so fruitful that he forthwith abandoned any further immediate attention to the straying of tangerine oranges.

For he was faced with an affair that was going to need planning, reconnaissance, persuasion, co-ordination, briefing—and strenuous nocturnal exercise. He would need the assistance of, he calculated, preferably three and ideally four physically well-developed members of the uniformed branch. Their detachment to his command would have to be authorized. The inevitable objections of their operational superiors would have to be overruled. The task-force would have to be assembled, transported, instructed and deployed. Mistakes, misunderstandings and mechanical breakdowns would have to be taken in his stride, if not in the stride of those specifically employed to rectify them.

The report which suddenly activated Mosley had come from the old lady who lived alone, who was notorious for walking her poodle whenever anything of interest seemed likely to break in her home village of Cresset, and who had become Mosley's firm friend ever after he had eased her over a completely misguided complaint that she had once made about a non-existent Peeping Tom who she believed had been spying on her ablutions from under her eaves. Mosley had always found her one of the most rewarding agents in his network, for amid her copious irrelevancies and capricious digressions the salient facts were always somewhere to be found, needing only the arts of an experienced interpreter.

In the present instance the crisp precision with which he had briefed her had done much in advance to shear away surplus material. It was perhaps inevitable that she believed that the newest young doctor in the group medical practice had been spying on her with binoculars from a high fork in an ancient beech tree. But, this apart, she was clear about the Cortina Estate car—G registration, and remainder of number-plate obligingly noted—which had lingered briefly in Cresset this morning. It had apparently mistaken its route, for it had proceeded only a few yards up the Giggleswick Road when it had stopped, attempted a reversing manoeuvre on the grass verge and become bogged down, its offside rear wheel digging itself deeper in with every revolution.

The driver had had to get out to go to a farm, Isaac Jowett's, to borrow a spade with which to extricate the vehicle. Isaac Jowett had, for the last two years, been fattening turkey-poults, what was known as running them on, on experimental sub-contract to a large-scale purveyor in Wakefield.

Mosley spent a large portion of the afternoon with the old lady who lived alone. He admired her home-made jams, and she had a propensity for producing home-made wines of epic potency at unorthodox drinking hours which it would have been tactless to have discouraged. He made diplomatic notes about all her manifold recent causes for alarm and left her before first dark to survey the theatre of tonight's encounter.

As compared with Neddy Sladburn's, Isaac Jowett's was a real farm, with modern machinery in evidence and the shed that housed the turkeys both visible and audible from the road. There was also a large metal skip containing the mortal remains of such sickly or over-pacific young poults as had failed in the struggle. Keeping this to leeward, Mosley approached Isaac Jowett, who appeared to believe that a battery of shotguns manned by himself, his sons and grandsons would be preferable to the time-consuming and ultimately unreliable processes of the law. Mosley was eventually able to decide on a course of action and—what was basic to it—the best use of ground. There had to be an area in which the thieves would be allowed to work unmolested until such time as they had burdened themselves with evidence against them. There had to be cover behind which the forces at Mosley's command could wait for the whistle; and there had to be scope for a pincer-movement which would turn attempted retreat into self-sacrifice.

Mosley decided all these elements in battle and set off for the rendezvous with his troops. These transpired, thanks to various urban priorities which obtruded themselves at the critical moment, to consist of one village constable, the incumbent of Cresset itself, a man within a month of retirement, in whom the beacon of ambition had burned down to a mere memory in the ash. Mosley posted him in a hedge-bottom from which, if not actually asleep, he might be able to observe the parking of the rustlers' transport. Himself, he went into the cover he had already chosen, a dense and thorny thicket from which he could see the main door of the turkey-house and the cinder-track leading up to it.

There were certain crimes, Mosley had always considered, in which the risk and physical labour were so great, the chances of discovery so probable, the discomfort so appalling and the rewards so uncertain that they could surely only be committed by romantics in love with misdemeanour and suspense for their own sake. Among these he counted the stripping of lead from exposed heights, the puncturing of strongholds with aging and unstable explosives and the acquisition of works of art which could not under any circumstances be displayed. As he settled down in his bed of thorns, with a growing suspicion that a wind of change was now blowing over the canister of carcases, he now added the purloining of livestock to his list of incomprehensibles.

The hour-hand of his wrist-watch pushed up towards

eleven. Ground-floor lights continued to burn behind the windows of the Jowett residence. He pictured three generations of Jowetts keeping their own counsel about his admonitions, the working parts of their shotguns clean, bright and slightly oiled. At a quarter past eleven the downstairs lights were extinguished and three upstairs windows showed pale yellow rectangles. At a quarter to midnight they were still showing. A motor vehicle drove at modest speed through the village, changed into low gear and cruised slowly past the entrance to the farm, picking up speed after inspection and driving off in the direction of Giggleswick. At least there was some hope that they would have wakened PC Hunter; but he wished he had a runner whom he could have sent to tell the Jowetts for God's sake to get their heads down. At a little after ten minutes past twelve he was alerted by an at first indefinable variation in the ongoing noises of the night. This was not a weasel. It was not an owl taking off from a branch. It was not a mouse among dry leaves: all the leaves, like his ankles, the turn-ups of his trousers and the inside of his coat-collar, wete wet. He pricked up his ears; but the car was coming back again down the Giggleswick Road and its engine played havoc with the local noise-to-signal ratio. Again it slowed down, but this time on brakes alone, not more than notionally. Again its driver must have taken note of the vigilance of the Jowetts, and again he drove off for more time.

But then Mosley heard again, and this time much nearer at hand, the anomalous sounds that had disquieted him not long ago; and wishful thinking could not dispel the only reasonable explanation. Someone was approaching him from behind. Of course, poachers were not unknown in the history of Cresset; nor were nocturnal fornicators or even the allowably enamoured. But this man was making too much noise for a poacher, yet taking too much care over his fieldcraft for one on his lawful occasions. There was a long pause, a patient suspension of movement, after every brush against a twig, every pebble set rolling. Once there were the unmistakable sounds of the man falling and Mosley could picture a heel losing its grip down the greasy slope of an unseen bank. There was a longer silence after that set-back; and in that interval the last of the Jowetts' lights suddenly went out. Mosley braced himself for action—but action on two fronts, he knew, lay outside his potential. He strained his ears afresh for any indication that the car was approaching.

He judged that the other oncomer was now not more than ten to fifteen yards behind him. There was a chance that he might even pass him in the dark and vanish on an oblique course towards his own business. But Mosley knew that this was unlikely. He himself, in order to permit rapid emergence, had avoided the more impenetrable parts of the thicket and was in the line of any man choosing a moderately carefree line of progress; Mosley had heard no evidence that the stranger was hacking his way with a *parang* or *yataghan*. And indeed, a second or two later, the new arrival had reached him. There was a sudden over-dramatized whisper.

'All right. Don't panic. It's me.'

'How interesting.'

'Sergeant Beamish. I gathered I'd find you in this neighbourhood. I want to talk to you about the Cryer case.'

'Ah. No time quite unlike the present.'

'They've put me on an aspect of it that's more up your street than mine.'

'Sh!'

But whatever Mosley had heard was lost on Beamish—who nevertheless respected the silence until Mosley spoke again.

'False alarm. They may not come back.'

'Bit thin on the ground, aren't you?'

'Your arrival has increased my reserves by a hundred per cent.'

'At your disposal. We'll get your bit of business out of the way before I go into mine.'

'Thank you.'

'Though you'd better not let Marsters or Grimshaw know I've been helping you.'

'Or even associating with me, I suppose?'

'It's not quite like that, Mr Mosley.'

'Sh!'

This time there was no mistaking it. It was not an isolated noise. It was the let's-get-it-over-with orgiastic outburst of a faction who were resigned to the inevitability of noise at this juncture. It came from the very far end, the blind side of the poultry-house, and it issued from lusty young turkeys awakened and pounced on pell-mell, from tearaway young turkeys escaping into the night, from less star-blessed young turkeys confined in sacks and carried over men's shoulders, from the pounding of those men's feet across a field, from the running-up of sash windows and the firing out of them of double barrels and from the haphazard showering of lead shot over corrugated iron roofs.

Beamish made to press forward out of the thicket.

'Don't be silly, Sergeant. We don't stand a chance. I took them for lazy men who'd be bound to park here, where they surveyed the ground this morning. As it is, they got tired of waiting for the sandman to clobber the Jowetts. So they switched to the back approach. Which means they've half a mile cross-country run to their nearest parking-point. And we don't stand an earthly.'

'We can alert mobile patrols.'

'We also have their car number and the Sheffield police can search them for feathers in the morning. That's what I'm settling for. Now what's all this about Brenda Cryer?'

'This seems hardly the best of places to talk.'

'What time is it?'

'A quarter to one.'

'Pubs won't be closed yet,' Mosley said. 'Not in this part of the world. Let's try the Anchor at Padbolt.'

Fourteen

'Marsters,' Beamish said, 'got his first inkling from a grass about two years ago. Not a super-grass, either. Just a bottom-of-the-dredger copper's nark, who hadn't got personal experience of what he was talking about, who'd got no backing for his word, and whose evidence would have raised hollow laughter in any jury-room.'

They had gained admittance to the Anchor, whose landlord had expressed the most inhospitable disgust at the sight of them. He had only just got rid of his domino school and between one and two in the morning was ready for bed. But he understood the last-ditch menace in Mosley's eye—a look such as he had never seen in the old man's eye before—and he resignedly stoked up the fire for them.

'Do we consider we're on duty?' Mosley asked.

'Absolutely not,' Beamish said. 'I've been warned you'd come plying me with questions about the Cryer case—which you haven't. And I've been told not to unbuckle a thing.'

'We'll have a couple of pints of best bitter, then. And then you can leave us to it, Joe Mycock.'

'Marsters's tip-off wasn't evidence,' Beamish said, 'and well he knew it. But it rang true. It was the sort of yarn an experienced copper believes. And Marsters put it away in the back of his mind, took it out now and then, gave it a dusting and looked it over. And it gathered strength as time passed. There were middle-of-the-road villains who were getting silks to their defence; bottom-of-the-barrel screwsmen who were going to work in strange company; wives of men who'd gone down still buying new furniture; men who were coming out to a spot of well-heeled leisure after they'd finished their time; bent coppers who were very choosey where they were doing their favours. There was nothing you could prove—above all else, there was nothing you could prove. But there were a lot of things that could be explained away if you played with the idea that somebody with a lot of money, and a lot of brains, and a lot of contacts, was organizing the aristocrats of the trade. It had to be somebody, too, who was enjoying the game, getting a kick out of tweaking well-chosen noses. I don't give Marsters much credit for spotting that Hartley Mason might fill the bill. If you ask me, it wouldn't have occurred to him if Mason hadn't wiped the witness-box rail with him in some quite insignificant case. It was police-court stuff, the pettiest of possible larcenies, and Mason got Marsters's man off on a technicality that made Marsters look a berk. It was only through childish malice that Marsters tried to see if he could fit Mason into this role of hypothetical manager: which was why he wasn't listened to in high places when he first started going on about it. But the odd thing was that Mason did fit—if you looked at him from the right angle. And what ultimately clinched it—and won Grimshaw over to Marsters's side—was a sort of dog-that-didn't-bark syndrome. You remember that chap Palfrey, who was sprung out of Aston, and they never did get to the bottom of it? The strange thing was that Hartley Mason had acted for him often enough in the past, had got him off a time or two—but hadn't represented him on the charge that he'd just gone down on. There could, of course, be plenty of possible reasons for that. But then Marsters hunted out another case. A little tyke breaker-and-enterer at Manchester Crown Court put up a QC who was quite out of his class, got acquitted. And he'd just sacked Hartley Mason, too—though in the past he'd always come running to him when he was in trouble. Marsters's theory was that Mason was getting rid of characters he didn't want to be associated with—but he was still pulling the strings behind the scenes.'

Mosley went behind the bar to the pumps and topped up both their tankards.

'Marsters followed up those lines. He watched where Mason was acting—and who he was ditching. And that very nearly splintered the theory, because Mason was too smart to be consistent. He dropped some, carried on with others. Marsters calls that a randomization of alibis.'

Mosley looked neither surprised nor complacent. He might have been a child, grown old before his years, who has suddenly been told that he is in a new world—and can see nothing different in it.

'Of course,' Beamish said, 'this all fitted in with Mason's existing image: the conceited junior partner of the long-standing firm. He was the one who first brought Fothergills into crime in a big way. It was a local trade at first. Then it spread over the north-west and into Yorkshire. Then he started picking up national figures. And what a cover he had! Solicitors aren't allowed to advertise, but Hartley Mason kept his name in front of the people who mattered to him: letters to the press, papers in professional periodicals, correspondence with MPs that got questions asked in the House. Mason on prison reform; Mason on the handling of suspects in police custody; Mason on deaths in overnight cells; Mason on diminished responsibility; Mason the canvasser of new legislation on the account-ability of Chief Constables—Mason, in fact, the national prisoner's friend. Which he also was in a lot of ways that he didn't advertise.'

Beamish was still young enough to be excited by a current case. Mosley did not stir. He did not look as if anything had ever moved him in his life.

'Marsters says it was like an army: an army that's owned by its field-marshal, a man who does his own staff-work. Mason has a vast intelligence department, an interlocking and cross-checked knowledge of money move-ments, of wage lifts, of art markets and outlets—and especially where money, blackmail or a fiddled privilege can buy one: prison warders, senior police, wallies on the beat, security guards, transport managers. He has his own technical services, an encyclopaedic knowledge of the right man for the right job. Sweaty and Jock, putting something together in Sunningdale, Berks, don't have to worry about who's going to get into the safe, who's going to do a spot of steeplejacking over the roof, what they are going to drive away in, who's going to buy the loot, what sun-drenched beach they're going to celebrate on: not if they've been admitted to Mason's élite. Above all, if they need to be capitalized, and Mason approves of the ploy, then they've no worries in that direction.'

'And can Marsters prove any of this?'

'What you do think? The more he dug around, the more convinced he became—yet he could still find nothing that they'd act on upstairs. So he changed his approach. Instead of trying to get at the warp and weft of the overall picture, he decided to follow up one case in depth, with all its ramifications, however trivial. And he found another parallel with a well-run army: the troops have to have confidence in the welfare arm. *When the enterprising burglar's not a-burgling, not a-burgling,* he has his wife and kids to think about. He might have the odd stretch to serve, either because he's unlucky or because the system has had to sacrifice him for some tactic or other. That has to be made worth his while. More important, he's got to know, while he's inside, that the little woman is getting better supplementary benefits than the government pays. In other words, there has to be a domestic back-up system, a left hand that might not know too much about right hand's activities, but that every man-jack in the ranks knows that he can rely on.'

Beamish took a draught of refreshment.

'Policemen need the odd stroke of luck as much as anyone else, and Marsters suddenly had one. There was a receiving and disposing ring based in Preston on which he'd done some of the fringe work. And one of the men who went down was a man called Frank Humberstone. Not much to reckon with. There are Humberstones doing bird all over the country, and not one of them ever amounted to much.'

'I had one up on my patch, once. I did him for pinching a crate of lemonade from a cricket pavilion.'

'That sounds like an average Humberstone operation. Anyway: Frank Humberstone went down, and about a month after the trial, Marsters caught sight of Mrs Humberstone, going into Fothergills. He loitered, because he was curious: the Humberstones lived in the Wirral, which is a long way from Bradburn. And Mrs Humberstone was visibly upset—a woman whose tether-ends were showing. She was arguing, volubly, with that gaunt woman at the reception desk: it didn't look as if she had an appointment—and she wasn't going to wait for one, either. But she did manage to get shown upstairs. The pattern was an interesting one—and familiar. Up to three years ago, Hartley Mason had invariably been Humberstone's mouthpiece. For this latest case, there'd been a change. Yet it was to Mason that Humberstone's wife turned when, as was obviously the case, there was some sort of trouble. Women!'

Beamish suddenly sounded like a man who'd had troubles of his own in that department.

'There has to be a weak link in every chain. No wonder management consultants have started interviewing executives' wives. I suppose you can't expect a woman in married quarters to have the same respect for the sergeant-major that her husband has. And that was another good reason, Marsters argued, why Mason would keep his welfare wing well screened off from the Operations Room. He kept a close eye on Mrs Humberstone, for the short time she was in Bradburn. She wasn't upstairs with Mason for long, came out evidently dissatisfied, even talking to herself under her breath. She went straight to the railway station and bought herself a ticket to Scarborough. Well: Marsters couldn't follow her there, but he got on the blower and asked Scarborough to run her to earth if they could. But they missed her. Marsters could really sniff the battlefield cordite now. He'd been keeping close tabs on Mason, and Mason was taking two or three winter weekend breaks a year over in Scarborough. But Scarborough was as far as Marsters had ever accounted for him. It took you to lay the trail to Ember Bay.'

'No—you,' Mosley said. 'You're the one who chipped out the dental records.'

'You got there first,' Beamish said, not unruefully. 'Anyway—Marsters sees it all now—or thinks he does— thanks to what you've unearthed. Hartley Mason knew Brenda from the time she was ministering unto old William— maybe he was even having it away with her on the side. When old William dies, leaving her unexpectedly destitute, all Mason can do is commiserate. As a lawyer, there's no help he can give her. Even an *ex gratia* payment is out of the question, due to cross-currents in the firm, and resentment by the Fothergill offspring. Then he suddenly sees an opening for her. She is a superb secretary; she probably did quite a lot of right-hand woman work for old William during those years in the Dales. She's seen her share of low life and has been neither contaminated nor thrown off-balance by it. She has roughed it and survived. She's been too badly let down in her time to take any more dicey chances with men. She has no love for the establishment. She's a soft spot for down-and-outs. She's got to support herself—and she's damned if she'll ever rely on another man. What better welfare officer— with a genuine but not over-trodden seaside hotel as her cover? A hotel that can be at once report centre, transit camp and safe house?'

'Possible,' Mosley said.

'You don't sound convinced.'

'I don't know, one way or the other. Has Marsters thought of everything? Are men perfect in this underworld Utopia of Hartley Mason's? Is there no such thing as disloyalty? What does he do when a Humberstone is just plain stupid? Suppose he doesn't approve of this Sunningdale job: are Sweaty and Jock going to go it alone? Suppose he likes the job, but doesn't think Sweaty and Jock are the ones to do it? Suppose some peterman is asked in to do a combination for them, and casually slips twenty thousand into his own inside pocket?'

121

'Marsters thinks Mason had a percentage contingency margin to cover human weaknesses.'

'Surely. But what if Mrs Humberstone thinks Sweaty's wife has had more than her share of holidays in Benidorm? Suppose Sweaty falls for an inducement, and grasses on Jock? These things need discipline from time to time. Even Hartley Mason needs a heavy mob.'

'Who's to say he hasn't one?'

'His reprisals would have to be memorable, if he wanted to keep the peace in his kind of empire. If it were my case, that's where I'd be moving in from.'

Beamish nodded appreciatively.

'That's what Marsters thinks, too. He thinks that Brenda was what you call a memorable reprisal. What's more memorable than murder? What's going to shake an army more than the knowledge that a Corps Commander has just had his? Brenda wanted out. Perhaps she just wanted a change. Or maybe there was another memorable reprisal, somewhere, which she'd heard of and didn't like the cut of. What better cover for her than to go home and nurse her own mother? That is the gospel according to Marsters. Marsters doesn't like you, by the way.'

'That's his privilege.'

'You stole a march on him for which he'll never forgive you. He had finally got authority to go and confront Mason. There were a lot more bits and pieces that I haven't mentioned to you—disconnected grounds for sus. He still didn't know about the Brenda connection, because he'd had no reason to rummage in William Fothergill's private life. He didn't know about Ember Bay. Yet you'd been chatting to Mason about those things two minutes before Marsters went into his office. He's convinced that you put Mason on his guard. Mind you, it's only in his hysterical moments that he suggests that may not have been an accident.'

Mosley did not seem outraged by the insinuation.

'I'm telling you this,' Beamish said, 'to show you frankly where I stand. I changed my mind about you, over in Ember Bay, you know.'

There was something almost schoolboyish about Beamish's step-by-step self-justification.

'I was impressed by what you dug out of Bay View. I liked the cut of your jib when we were burgling. I was impressed by the way you handled old Mrs Thwaites. I'm impressed by the grip you've got over this private bloody wilderness of yours. And I want you working with me. Marsters doesn't seriously think you're one of Mason's satellites. Grimshaw, if that's any comfort to you, refuses to listen to him when he talks like that. But they are in agreement to keep you out of things, just in case—and I'm quoting them—you mess something else up.'

Mosley was not offended.

'So they've given me the job of tapping the gossip in Parson's Fold—even of going over for another session with old Mrs Thwaites. You'd do both jobs better than any man they could turn to.'

Mosley showed neither pleasure nor irritation at this effusive and naive expression of confidence, so out of place between professional colleagues that Beamish would have been branded a crawler in some company.

'Mind you,' Beamish said, 'if you feel at all uneasy about conflicting with higher authority—'

Mosley laughed heartily.

'The key question, to which they want an answer tomorrow, is whether Hartley Mason was one of the visitors that Brenda received at Jackman's Cottage. If they can establish that, they feel that they'll have case enough to have him in and talk to him till he's tired.'

'They'll trip up if they do,' Mosley said.

'You talk as if you know something.'

'No more than anyone else would, who'd given his mind to it.'

'Well—what about it? If we were to bump into each other, by accident, in Parson's Fold, do you think you could have found time to chat up a few of your old friends?'

'Quid pro quo.'

'Anything you like.'

'I've a case I'd like taken off my hands.'

'If I can possibly fit it in.'

'It won't take you long. Only a crate of bloody oranges. To tell you the truth, it's beginning to get on my wheel. I suppose I'd better get off now and ring night-duty at Sheffield and get them looking for turkey-feathers.'

He said nothing about his conversation with Neddy Sladburn; did not mention that the car-breaker had met Mason at Jackman's.

Fifteen

Mosley, as they parted that night, had been difficult to nail down about the details of their meeting the next day.

'Oh, some time between ten o'clock and half past two,' he said, so seriously that he seemed to mean it.

'Where, then?'

'Somewhere around.'

Ten o'clock seemed well advanced in the day to a man of Beamish's energies: time to dispose of the small affair of the Spritwell oranges. By half past nine, having followed up every lead that Mosley had given him, he was beginning to doubt his own sanity. Alice Renshaw, the elderly assistant who had had charge of the greengrocer's shop since it had opened at eight, looked upon every question he asked her as a slight upon her honesty. The shopkeeper, Peter Morridge, who arrived at a quarter to nine, bringing in the day's supply from a wholesaler on the back seat of his family car, was a vague, repetitive and dogmatic man who by now thoroughly regretted having reported the theft in the first place. He and Mrs Renshaw answered questions in operatic duo, with long explanatory digressions in which no issue was simple. Beamish asked to see the original invoice for the fruit, which suddenly could not be found. The day of the loss, it seemed, had been a heavy one for Lower Spritwell, greengrocery-wise: there had been a hamper made up for a raffle prize at the Pigeon

Club; a bedside basket to go up to the hospital. Beamish wandered into the village street, where there was no lack of informants: only a lack of information. Beamish, struggling hard not to be abrasive—for all these villagers were surely Mosley's friends—began to feel that he was losing his touch.

He drove down to Parson's Fold, the Spritwell oranges no nearer to accountability than Mosley had left them. And in Parson's Fold a very opposite spirit prevailed from the tangled helpfulness of Spritwell. Here people were not falling over themselves to answer questions. There did not even seem to be any people. There were no comings and goings this morning. The pub was not yet open. The wooden bench round the oak tree was unoccupied. Kitchen doors were shut, their panels conveying an impression of prolonged domestic coma. Women were not gossiping; there were no women in evidence. The children had been bussed off to school. And those of pre-school age, whom one might expect to have found playing with dangerous farm machinery and sucking their fingers on dunghills, appeared to have been locked into cellars and coalholes. Somebody with a good pair of eyes and a faultless memory for his number-plate must have spotted Beamish while he was still dust on the horizon.

At least the peace of the village assured him of an uninterrupted session in Jackman's Cottage, a dream which had so far been denied him. And even in his wave of admiration for the inspector, he had not forgiven Mosley for the cavalier fashion in which he had despised the scientific evidence on the spot. Beamish loved scientific evidence—though even in the enlightened home-ground of his Q Division, he had not so far made his name by inferring miracles from it.

He stood now in the living-cum-sickroom and steeped himself in the thought that this was a room in which murder had happened. A room in which murder had happened was not quite the same as a room which had not witnessed a killing. In the more reasonable type of ghost story, the explanation was sometimes put forward that, in some way not yet accounted for, places could register emotions and energies, playing them back at random to visitors with the right grade of sensitivity. Beamish stood for some seconds to see what vestiges of recorded distress his own sensibility could pick up in here. The result was akin to switching on a record-player during a power-cut; or maybe he had the wrong type of stylus. This was a sickroom which had been untidily vacated. It was a living-room in which no fire had been lit for the last ten days—with autumn eroding the days and a chill—an early frost, even—staking a claim in the nights. It was a room in which no one had flicked a duster since before the killing, in which objects had been moved, drawers unpacked and repacked by policemen with other work to hurry away to. Nevertheless, it was a room in which murder had been done—in the presence of these armchairs, those pictures, those china ornaments.

Fainter than before Mosley had trampled over it, there was the chalk-line that marked where the body had lain. Beamish studied it systematically. Given the woman's weight and height and the pathologist's record of bruises sustained in falling, it should be possible to work out the position in which she had been standing when the shot was fired. Beamish got out the photograph of Brenda Cryer's body, lying *in situ.* Both the lie of the corpse and his own interpretation of her fall suggested that she might suddenly have swung round, have turned her back on her killer. So where had he been standing? Behind her—when her back was towards him. That was so obvious, it had to be bloody silly. Though even the obvious, he told himself, was worth thinking over at this stage. *At this stage?* Wasn't it high time they pushed on a stage or two?

The medical report had attested what any layman who could bear to look would have seen with his naked eye: that the little bijou pistol had been fired only an inch or two from the nape of the neck. So he had been in the same room as her; so he was probably someone whose presence had not unduly alarmed her: she had probably been talking to him at the time. So why had she turned round to enable him to shoot her? Had he played some puerile *What's that?* prank on her, and she had swung her torso? And his fingers had perhaps already been clasped round his pistol, perhaps in his trousers pocket. He had held it an inch from her cervical vertebrae and fired.

Could it have been otherwise? Was that in question?

Beamish got out Forensic's report and read it again—the first time he had read it in the actual room, though he knew it by heart from office perusal. They all knew it by heart from office perusal—Grimshaw and Marsters, and everyone with a shred of suspected specialism in his makeup to whom it had been referred for an opinion. It had not been referred for Beamish's opinion. Beamish had had to ask to see it.

It was a careful report, exhausting all the available evidence. Dust had been analysed from the soles, welts and laceholes of Brenda's shoes, from the hems and seams of her slacks. Scrapings had been taken from her fingernails, her scalp and the holes pierced for her ear-rings. Comparisons had been made with garden soil, mantel-dust and beatings out of the upholstery. And the only thing that was proven to the point of certainty, forensic scientists being the positivists that they were, was that Brenda Cryer had lived in Jackman's Cottage during the period in which it was already known that she had. Beamish did his best to prevent himself from becoming disenchanted with Forensic; of course, science had its limitations—though that was no excuse for Mosley's ignoring it altogether.

At opening time, Beamish went across to The Crumpled Horn. At opening time The Crumpled Horn opened, and those gentlemen who were always there were there. Unlike the outdoor village, they did not treat Beamish to silence. They treated him as if they knew him well, admired his record and wished strength to his arm; and they skilfully avoided saying anything that was worth his hearing. One old fellow called Arthur Blamire left his pint, saying that he was nipping back home for a minute or two to put a light under his potatoes.

Beamish knew—and with fear—that once he had compromised the line that he had come to the village to pursue, then that line was compromised. This was a morning, it seemed, for the elegantly obvious; once the damage was done, it was done. Beamish hardly dared make a start: a rare attitude for him. Then, like a learner making his first dive, he dived.

'Everywhere I go, I keep hearing stories about visitors calling on Brenda Cryer, when she moved back to Jackman's—'

And such a blunt introduction produced a silence at first, a sort of community concussion.

'Everybody seems to know about it,' Beamish said, 'yet no one can name names.'

'Aye, well, there used to be an old saying about that,' someone put in at last. 'Something to do with pack-drill, if I remember correctly.'

Beamish realized that they had to be put at their ease. 'No one's saying anything about pack-drill. We're not going to arrest the first person we know to have gone in there. But somebody could tell us something—if only we knew whom to ask.'

It sounded appallingly weak. They chewed it over— and to them, apparently, it sounded appallingly sinister. No one could think of anything to say at all. They were trying, of course, to make Beamish himself name a name, thereby undermining himself irrevocably.

'If only we could speak to someone who'd set foot in there—'

'Like the milkman?'

'No, of course we know what he has to say. Someone— well, someone who might have used his eyes. Someone you wouldn't perhaps have expected to call there.'

And then a man in a corner laughed. 'Shall I tell you what I think? I reckon it's old Arthur Blamire you ought to be talking to. He's in and out of here like a jack-in-the-box, always reckoning to have something to put on the hob or take off it. Maybe he fancied his chances up at Jackman's.'

'Or else it was Stevie Pollitt.'

Gross and universal laughter. Beamish did not know who Stevie Pollitt was, but it was clear that he was either the village idiot or some decrepit elder statesman. He was surprised that with the woman not long dead, there should have been this willingness to lapse into crude humour about her. It suggested two things: firstly, that there was at bottom a standing contempt for her reputation; secondly that they were solidly unwilling to commit themselves on the side of authority.

Then Arthur Blamire came back.

'Just the man we want, Arthur. Your ears been burning, have they? Your name's being taken in vain, Arthur.'

And Blamire looked round their faces with puzzlement and anxiety; an unintelligent and lonely old widower.

'You spend more time crossing the road than you do either at home or in here, Arthur. The detective wants to know who you saw visiting at Jackman's.'

'What—while Brenda was there?'

Goodness knows why else he thought Beamish might be interested.

'Oh—I can tell you who that was.'

And Beamish looked at him with a hopefulness that seemed to be shared by everyone in the room.

'I said to myself—I'd nipped back home, you know, because I had to keep pulling the chain, because of a worn washer in the ball-cock—I said to myself, now I wonder who's that, gone up there?'

He seemed to regard that as answering the question.

'And who was it?'

'Her brother,' he said, 'and his wife.'

Beamish gave up. At eleven o'clock he left the pub, decided to retreat back to Jackman's, where he could at least sit down. But as he was crossing The Pightle, he saw a tractor approaching, driven by a wild-looking man with a long-outgrown basin-cut sticking out all round from under his hat. Behind the tractor was a trailer, and in the trailer sat Mosley. He waved with great pleasure at the sight of the sergeant.

'Can we go up to the cottage first?' he asked as he got down. 'I've thought of one or two things that I didn't do justice to, last time I was in there.'

So they went up to Jackman's and it looked for some time as if Mosley was doing precisely what Beamish had done: weighing up niceties of evidence to which he hadn't paid much attention before.

'You don't happen to have the forensic report on you?'

Beamish produced it and Mosley studied it, apparently with growing perplexity. But he did not communicate any of his findings, either about the report or the room. Instead he said, 'Mind if I take another general look-round?' and went through each of the other rooms in turn. Beamish heard him go upstairs, and presently he reappeared, carrying an armful of old clothes.

'Some people are strange, aren't they? I mean, they had this place up for sale, and yet they still haven't cleared all the drawers and wardrobes. I can understand them holding on to the stuff while the old girl was still living here—she was probably as sentimental as hell about it. But this is a good coat—'

Mosley laid a heavy dark overcoat over the arm of a chair. It was not new, but it had not been worn often. There was also a narrow-brimmed bowler hat, of the quality that is the hallmark of a certain fastidious type of professional man; and a faultlessly furled umbrella. When old Thwaites was made managing clerk, he knew precisely what image to step into.

'And this, I imagine, is the sort of thing that a devoted family might give a man on his sixtieth birthday.'

This was an expensive and fashionable executive briefcase.

'You'd have thought, wouldn't you, that young Thwaites would have taken this for his own use? But I suppose there's some sort of sentimental barrier there, too.'

Mosley went through every pocket and compartment in the case, but the thing had been efficiently cleared. There was one postage-stamp of pre-decimal vintage.

'Does this tell us anything?' Beamish asked.

'It tells us about a certain attitude to death; about an unwillingness to face up to it—even to think about it afterwards. Possibly we shall be told that young Thwaites simply did not have time to dispose of his father's effects— that he kept putting it off till next week. There are other things up there, too. Perhaps it was the old woman who insisted on hanging on to everything—and after she went, they never got round to it.'

'I don't see that this can possibly be relevant.'

'Everything's relevant, Sergeant, that tells us anything about anyone. Anyway, I want to hang on to these few things myself for the time being. All right—don't look so worried—I'll give you a receipt for them.'

'I'm not very good at riddles this morning, Mr Mosley.'

'Hat, coat, umbrella, case: I've got a use for these things, if the murderer takes the line of action I think he will.'

'This is beyond me.'

'It shouldn't be. Have you sorted out those oranges for me yet?'

Beamish groaned.

'All right, Sergeant, let's pay a call. I'd like to get my feet inside the Old Rectory again.'

So they walked together past the lawn that could have competed with an Oxford quadrangle. But Beryl Thwaites looked rather less academic than the Vice-Chancellor of an ancient university. She had on a vast and shiny plastic apron bearing the reproduction of a historic poster advertising an apparently pre-Raphaelite soap. Her hair was wrapped in a drab cloth, her nail-varnish was palpably unrenewed and she had deployed in her spacious entrance hall the not inconsiderable range of accessories that went with her vacuum cleaner. Her pretence that she was not displeased to see them came a little belatedly.

'I'm sorry. You've caught me on a bad morning. I'm having a spring-clean. Donald has gone to Ember Bay to fetch Mother. We are fixing up a downstairs room for her. We are not going to let her go back into any of those horrible homes.'

'You mean, your husband has taken a day off from work?'

'He has more than a day owing to him, Mr Mosley.'

'That I don't doubt. Well, in that case, Mrs Thwaites, I wouldn't dream of trespassing on your time.'

'Oh, but if I can be of any help—'

'No, really.'

Mosley turned on his heel and Beamish's feet were on the verge of following his example when the inspector had a second thought.

'You could help me on one little point if you would.'

Mrs Thwaites looked all readiness.

'Who is the Company Secretary at your husband's works?'

It was a simple little question, in casual enough tone, and although Beamish could not see what bearing it had on the case, he did not miss the effect that it had on Mrs Thwaites. She did not actually catch her breath, she did not markedly blush: but it was clearly a question that she neither expected nor relished. Her lower lip lost its discipline for a second.

She looked first sharply at Mosley, and then away from him. 'You mean one of the personal secretaries?'

'No: I mean the Company Secretary—the board's right hand.'

'Why, that's Pauline Murray, wife of one of the directors.'

'Ah, yes. I could have got that out of one of the standard directories, of course.'

'Why, what—?'

'Oh, it's nothing, really—just a thought. I wonder if you'd allow me to use your telephone?'

And Beamish thought that this was just an excuse to get their feet into the house, so that Mosley could ask any questions he wanted to, irrespective of what he had said about not hindering her.

But all he did was to ring up Murray and Paulson's, work his way round their switchboard to somebody helpful, and make an appointment to see Mrs Murray an hour from now. And as soon as he had put the receiver back down on its rest, he dialled again, a number which Beamish was surprised to see he carried in his head. But the nature of the call that he made was more than a surprise: it was a positive shock.

'I want an appointment, please, to see Mr Hartley Mason—but not in his office. I'd like to meet him in his home—or anywhere else he would care to suggest. This evening: yes—that would be fine. Drinks before dinner: that is a very civilized way of doing business.'

Mosley put down the receiver again as if challenging Beamish to point to any irregularity.

'My God,' Beamish said as they walked back along the drive. 'I'm not supposed to have brought you here. I'm not supposed to have whispered a word about the case. If Marsters finds out you've been talking to Mason again—'

'Oh, he'll find out. He might even in the long run have cause to be grateful—though I doubt if he'll have the manners to show it. You're right, though: it wouldn't do for him to find out too soon. That's why I made the appointment in Mason's home.'

'And he was ready to see you—without throwing up difficulties?'

'Of course. Don't you think he *knows* that the pincers are closing?'

'Well, this is something I think I'd better not know about, old friend. If you don't mind—'

'As you wish. I'd have thought, though, that Marsters would have preferred you to come with me. To keep me on the rails, so to speak. And, of course, to fill him in on what's been happening.'

Beamish unlocked his car, the passenger door first.

'You're a clever old bugger, aren't you? I wish I could be certain you're not overstepping it this time.'

'You wanted to know whether Mason was one of those who called on Brenda at the cottage. That was your brief, wasn't it?'

'Yes. But we don't seem to have moved any nearer to that simple issue.'

'We will. We'll ask Mason this evening, shall we?'

'And another thing I don't understand,' Beamish said, 'is where's the sense in the Thwaiteses bringing the old woman back to live with them?'

134

'Do you mean the sense in it—or the reasoning behind it?'

'Call it anything you like; it doesn't add up. The Thwaiteses can't stand the sight of her, nor she of them. Their home-life, their social round, for whatever that's worth, are going to be wrecked. And can you see Beryl Thwaites being nice to her?'

'No,' Mosley said. 'Life's going to be hell all round.'

'What, then?'

'You haven't grasped what makes the Thwaiteses tick.'

'Illusions—and not the sort that would appeal to any normal person.'

'On the contrary: the commonest clockwork spring behind most human actions, Sergeant—public opinion. Their image—not what people see of them, but what they think people see of them. They got by before, when the old girl was in The Towers, because everything just went quiet. Distance and oblivion, so they thought, so they kidded themselves, were saving them from public disgrace. But now there's been all this publicity, they can *see* the fingers pointing. And short of moving out of the village altogether—which would make fatal inroads into capital— they've simply got to do the right thing. They've got to be seen to be doing it. What is more—'

Mosley slewed round in the passenger seat and peered down a side-road; they were making a right-hand turn. He did not back-seat drive, but one would have thought that he did not trust his driver.

'What is more, Sergeant, that's why Brenda Cryer is dead.'

They went to Murray and Paulson's: it was by no means as easy to find parking space as it had been when Mosley had cycled in after working hours. Reception staff had clearly been alerted to expect them, and they were shown at once to Mrs Murray's office. It was the one whose door had stood slightly open when Mosley had come away from his first talk with Thwaites. It was the one through whose window a woman in heavy plum-red costume had been watching him as he tested his tyre-pressures with his thumb.

Mrs Murray was not wearing plum-red this morning. She was in off-white slacks that clung tightly to her fat thighs, emphasized without exaggerating the protuberance of her overfed buttocks. Her hair had been disposed of into a hasty French roll and she was wearing a blue ceramic brooch on a chain over a beige sweater in heavily ribbed knitwear. A far from comely woman; and no sign that she had ever been or desired to be one. Presumably she had at some time meant something to her husband. Presumably, from a different angle, she still did, for her shelves were up to date with Company Law, Trade Year Books, EEC Directories. Her command of the economics of small paint-trading was probably empirical, unadventurous, inelastic—and fundamentally sound. Murray and Paulson probably owed it largely to her nagging insistence on a few safe principles that they continued to exist on the perimeters of profitability.

'I don't know, gentlemen, in what respect you think I might be able to help you.'

'A quick answer to an unexpected question,' Mosley said, making the most of the enigma, though in a casual and entirely unsinister tone.

'Please ask me your question.'

'I just wondered whether you had noticed, during the last week or two, that someone has been following you.'

The question was certainly unexpected, and it certainly hit her. But she suppressed all but an initial revelation of the shock; presumably she had learned to keep her aplomb during what passed for sticky moments in the family board-room.

She laughed in the most humourless and unconvincing manner. '*Following* me? You mean men with their hatbrims pulled down over their eyes? Men leaping into taxis when they see me cross a road? This is a paint-factory, Mr Mosley, not a cover-plant for germ-warfare.'

Mosley seemed not to hear this at all. He simply sat waiting for an answer to his main question. When it

136

became obvious that she hoped to ridicule it away, he became quietly solemn. 'I'm afraid this is not a joke, Mrs Murray. It is a long story and, alas, not compounded of fancy. It could have lamentable consequences. That is why I want you to think hard, and see if you can remember anything unusual.'

She thought—or pretended to think. 'Somebody following me? It seems so improbable. And yet—'

'And yet, Mrs Murray—?'

'Well, no—there can't be anything in it. Two or three mornings last week, when I was leaving home to come here, there was a green van coming out of a side-road. And I noticed it again, a time or two—oh, just in the traffic, when I was coming home.'

'A green van?'

'The sort of thing a man might have bought tenth-hand. Dark streaks where a tradesman's name had been roughly painted out.'

'Did you catch sight of the driver?'

'Not at all. What is this about, Mr Mosley?'

'I don't think you need worry yourself, Mrs Murray. This is as we expected, and we have it in hand. But there is one more question—'

'Please ask me anything you like.' She looked bewildered. 'Anything to get this kind of thing off my shoulder.'

'I would like to know whether you have been away at all, on business trips, with Mr Donald Thwaites.'

'What are you getting at? What is this, Mr Mosley?' There was no doubting her disturbed state now.

'I am not getting at anything. I just want to establish a yea-or-nay fact. Have you been away at all, on business trips—?'

'I don't see of what possible interest it can be to you. But yes, I have.' She was not sheltering behind anger. 'He and I—and, I may add, a duenna from the typing pool, went to Cologne last March, in connection with a tender that is only just now coming to fruition.'

'You were away long?'

'Three nights, two working days, if you need to know.'

'Your husband did not accompany you?'

'He is managing director, Mr Mosley, and the works manager was down with a bug at the time. And if you are suggesting—'

'I am suggesting nothing. I have put a simple question of fact and you have answered it.'

She was summoning up kinetic forces inside her, like a clock that knows noon is approaching. Mosley thanked her, and they came away.

'Ghastly woman,' Mosley said, as they got back into the car. 'Though capable of getting and giving satisfaction, one is compelled to conclude. A man would need to be married to someone like Beryl Thwaites to look for adulterous relief there. God: I wonder what Murray's like?'

Sixteen

Hartley Mason might have been expected to have risen to at least a modest country property. He lived, in fact, on the outskirts of Bradburn, within walking distance of his office, in a largish post-Second War house set in largish though manageable grounds. They were indeed very well managed: a mature shrubbery, with exotic specimens, a grass tennis-court for his adolescent offspring, a loggia overlooking fishpond and fountain. But Mason was not a man who retreated to weekends of expansive leisure. He had a houseful of books—working books—and Beamish was impressed by the evidence of work in progress: a large stack of manuscript on a desk, with two works of reference open and a stack of others waiting with pages marked. Mason was evidently a man who improved all his shining moments.

Moreover, he was unexpectedly quite delighted to see Mosley.

'And may I say, Inspector, how much I appreciate your discretion in coming out here? There has been at least one official visit too many at the office. Malignant observers are beginning to invent things. What can I offer you gentlemen to drink?'

And, 'No,' he said, when the soda was tickling the Scotch, 'much as I admire zeal, perspicacity and unshackled imagination, I fear that your colleague Marsters is embarrassingly assiduous. And he is, I suspect, unaware of your present visit?'

'Quite so,' Mosley said, the archaism not strange from his lips.

'Not that I would have much difficulty in refuting the absurd charges which I fear the Chief Inspector is about to frame—but it would be a bore and a great waste of time to have to do so. The attendant publicity would not go down well with some of my partners. What is more, I fear that he is about to unearth something that I would far rather not have exposed to the broad light of day.'

'That I can well believe,' Mosley said, though with no sense of accusation.

'May I ask what put you on to it, Inspector?'

'You know there are things that I would not dream of asking you, sir—'

'You can always *ask*, Inspector.'

'Well, in that case, you wouldn't mind telling me, perhaps, what sort of a job it was that Brenda Cryer wanted you to set Matty Pearson on.'

'Now how on earth can you have got on to that? Don't tell me: it was that damned second-hand car-dealer. He had the look of an eavesdropper. Well, Inspector Mosley, I must simply remind you of the privileged relationship enjoyed by solicitor and client.'

'Yes, sir. I respect that. I will withdraw the question.'

Silence: and the potential of the interview seemed suddenly spent.

'Of course, sir, if you don't care to tell me, I dare say that Chief Inspector Marsters will be asking you the same question. Tomorrow, I wouldn't be surprised.'

Mason showed the hint of an appreciative grin. 'You're not suggesting that Marsters doesn't yet *know*?'

'I don't see how he can,' Mosley said innocently. 'His enquiries haven't taken him as far as hillside car-breakers yet.'

'You really are a bastard, Mosley. Didn't I once tell you that in open court?'

'Not in so many words, sir. But if you follow the way I am thinking, by being frank now, you might be able to save yourself a good deal of—what's the vogue word? —aggro?—in the comparatively near future.'

'You can call Marsters off?'

'Hardly that, sir.'

Mosley seemed to derive no end of amusement from the suggestion.

'But when I lay things on the line, sir, I dare say he will call himself off.'

'Or be called off by the Chief Constable?'

'That might happen *in extremis*. I always think these things are best done on a family level.'

Beamish had to fight not to wriggle. It was the nearest he had ever stood to stage-wing corruption. He had heard stories, of course, but had never had reason to suspect his own top corridor. And as for Mosley—!

'All right, Mosley. You have to win. Matty Pearson, as you know, is a private eye to be reckoned with. Let us say I have put him in once or twice to cut case-work corners for me.'

In fact, ninety per cent of Pearson's work came from Fothergills.

'I can't quite remember how Brenda came to know about him. I expect his name had cropped up some time when we were yarning.'

Oh, yes? How many briefings had Pearson had in Bay View?

'She wanted me to set him on to her brother.'

Mason was holding his glass at an angle looking into it as if he could see fairy pictures. *gova!*

'A squalid business—just about as nauseatingly uncompelling as anything you could think up. Donald Thwaites was supposed to have done some hotel-corridor tiptoeing with his boss's wife. The thought of that pair together is about as repellent an image as my mind could boggle at. Be that as it may, there are supposed to have been high jinks in Germany, and they sometimes stay late at the office: passionate panting behind the paint-pots. Never mind the sordid tableaux. They must need each other pretty badly. Or shall we say, each needs someone. All Brenda wanted to be able to do was to taunt him. He always took such a high-minded view of her own little side-histories. I don't know whether you've picked up Brenda's high sense of fun—especially when there's a neat twist of poetic justice in the tail.'

'And Matty Pearson delivered the goods?'

'Enough of them.'

The interview closed a few minutes after that.

Hartley Mason stood up to show them out. 'One thing occurs to me, Mosley. If you want a little evidence that will help you to convince Marsters, I dare say I can put you on to something.'

'That might be very helpful indeed.'

'Call at the front desk late tomorrow afternoon. I'll have something waiting for you.'

Beamish hardly felt able to talk to Mosley as they came away.

Seventeen

There was the rest of the day to kill; above all else, Mosley put it firmly into words, it was to be killed out of reach of headquarters. He himself disappeared into his hill-country, mumbling about the activities of mice in the absence of cats. He recommended Beamish to have a mechanical breakdown, preferably off the public highway. He suggested an abandoned quarry in which his car might be concealed.

But Beamish was to rematerialize at first twilight. He was to park his car in Parson's Fold, pointing the right way to be driven off without hindrance. He was to proceed to the Old Rectory, was to contrive to get and keep the three Thwaiteses in one room, and was to concentrate on questioning the old woman.

Beamish did not jib verbally, but his face was expressive.

'Go on!' Mosley told him. 'You're capable of holding the Thwaiteses in conversation, I hope. *Invent*, man! You'll get nowhere in this job if you can't keep the drama going.'

'But what am I to talk to the old woman *about*? Last time, we talked about rescuing sheep out of holes, being stuck out all night on the moors and flagging down passing conveyances.'

'In that case, tell her about other phenomenal sheep-rescues you've pulled off. Keep going out of the front door to see if a conveyance is coming. Above all else, keep her mind centred on the old days. Talk about her husband. Admire the man. Regret the passing of such prudence and decency. Adopt a reactionary attitude. Be on the side of the ancient battalions. I want her mind, such as it is, dwelling on a vanished security by the time I get there.'

'And when will that be?'

'I'll be along.'

And Mosley vanished hillwards to the empire of his capering mice before there could be any argument. It was in a state veering on misery that Beamish realized that he must either comply or abjure any further co-operation. And at the stage which things had now reached, that was out of the question. It was remarkable how firmly Mosley had him in the palm of his idiotic hand.

Beamish idled an afternoon away out of sight. As the light began to fail, he drove leisurely—an astute observer might have thought reluctantly—down to the Fold. He parked his car tidily under the oak, crossed The Pightle and strode, assuming an air of purpose at last, down to the Old Rectory.

Donald Thwaites came to the door to him, in broken-down maroon bedroom slippers and a formless cardigan, his clouded eyes peering out at the figure framed in the dusk. Beryl Thwaites had also advanced into the hall, unable to quell curiosity—and either not bothering to, or incapable of hiding her exasperation when she saw who their visitor was. The mother had not been put to bed yet, but was swaddled in rugs only a few feet in front of a blazing log fire, into which she was staring as if unaware that anyone else had come into the room.

'There are one or two little points I want to run over—mostly matters for confirmation or elimination.'

And Beamish had in fact worked out a programme of innocuous questions with which to get going, until such time as he saw the chance to bring Mrs Thwaites Senior into the conversation. But after a few minutes, he wondered whether this was going to be possible at all. She simply sat looking into the flames; perhaps she thought someone was roasting a sheep.

'Now you say that it was on the evening of the 17th that you had supper at Jackman's Cottage. I would like you to cast your minds back—'

Where the hell had Mosley got to? Three quarters of an hour plugged solidly by. Beamish decided to give him another ten minutes by the mock-ormolu clock.

'You heard rumours of male visitors to the cottage. Did any of the rumour-mongers advance theories about the actual personalities?'

The Thwaiteses must have suspected by now the repetitive purposelessness of it all. And still the old woman was present only as a blanketed hulk. Then suddenly there was a racket outside the front door: not a knocking or a ringing at the bell, but a veritable assault, as if someone were actually fighting the timbers. Then knocker and bell were attacked simultaneously. Thwaites and his wife looked afraid; even the old woman became aware that something was going on, looking from the fire into the body of the room for the first time.

Beamish went with Thwaites to the door. Thwaites opened it, and standing there was an angrily gesticulating man whom even Beamish did not at first recognize as Mosley. Mosley was wearing old Arthur Thwaites's narrow-brimmed professionally modish bowler, carrying Thwaites's rolled umbrella and birthday-present brief-case and wearing Thwaites's heavy, dark overcoat which, being on the long side for him, gave him a ridiculous and seedy-looking air.

But he carried this off by the sheer aggression of being unaware of it.

'Does a man have to wait to be let into his own house?'

And he came, blinking, appearing to totter slightly, in through the middle of the room.

'Arthur!'

Although the others, once the first shock was over, were not under any illusion, the old woman seemed completely taken in. Mosley put his hand to his forehead, stood still, looked as if he were about to reel.

'Donald—get a chair for your father. Can't you see he's not well?'

And such was the compelling nonsense of the scene that Donald Thwaites actually did this—moved an armchair in the direction of Mosley.

But Mosley, as Arthur Thwaites, had other things on his mind. Clumsily, snatching, he tore open the briefcase, brought out a large brown envelope and drew from it a handful of typescript.

'Just look at this—the shamelessness of it—to think that my daughter—'

He thrust the papers into the old woman's lap. Her eyes flickered over the lines as if she were reading them. 'Donald—just look at this—' She stretched out her arm, holding the documents out towards her son.

Thwaites took them, glanced briefly, then showed that he, at least, was refusing to take any more part in the pantomime. There was a light akin to frenzy in his yellowish eyes.

Mosley took two strides across to him and seized the papers from his hand. 'Well—so much for that!' And he threw the sheets into the heart of the fire, where they curled up one by one as the flames took the edges and corners. Mosley now put both hands to his head and began to sway.

'Cut it out, Mosley!'

Donald Thwaites had been pushed as far as he was going to allow. And as if obeying a parade-ground instruction, Mosley at once reverted to his proper self.

'But I didn't go far wrong, did I?'

'What's the point, anyway?'

'As you say—what's the point?'

Mosley turned to Beamish. 'When Arthur Thwaites visited his employer in a North Yorkshire property, he made the discovery, shocking to him, that his daughter was old William's mistress. And old William had meant this to happen. He had made a generous settlement on the girl, and he was convinced that a sight of that settlement would be a neutralizing comfort to anyone as steeped in the reliability of the law as his chief clerk. And one of

146

Arthur Thwaites's duties that afternoon was to bring the documents back to the office and file them away in old William's personal file, in William's personal safe. But William had sadly misread Arthur. He must have known about the narrowness of his attitudes and the limitations of his outlook—but he probably just didn't believe that they went as far as they did. Arthur Thwaites's daughter had her rewards still to come: and her father threw her title to them on to the fire. And you, Donald Thwaites, having read through those papers, watched him do it. You, Beryl Thwaites, had the greatest satisfaction in knowing that your sister-in-law would never be in a position to outdo you.'

Mosley swung round on Thwaites, and it seemed to Beamish that his indignation now was no mere acting.

'That was what your sister never forgave you for. Because you *knew*; and if only you had told her, she could have had the will drawn up again, have seen that it was properly safeguarded. But there's a streak of poisonous righteousness in you, Thwaites. As I say, Brenda never forgave you. Why should she? And when she found that she had it in her means to blackmail you, she had no second thoughts about it. She was going to give you hell. What chance would you have now of a seat on the board—even of keeping your present job—if certain facts were made known to the Managing Director? What chances, even, of finding another job, when the hard core of your experience has been nothing more up-to-date than Murray and Paulson's?'

Mosley let his eyes wander over to Beryl Thwaites, who was looking on now with fear, but without understanding.

'Do I have to go into the details in full, here and now?' Mosley asked.

Thwaites closed his eyes. It was as if everything had shut down on him. He was too lost and too tired to fight back at this clutch of circumstance—one of those criminals unable to carry anything off beyond the first heat of impulse.

'The trouble is,' Mosley said, 'it's been thought all

along, though in fact never put in words, that a lady's handbag pistol belongs in the world in which your sister spent much of her adult life. In fact, nothing is further from the truth. Anyone can get hold of a gun these days, if he really wants to. I don't care particularly how you came by it, Thwaites. I do want to know where it is now.'

Thwaites's shoulders moved involuntarily, but he said nothing.

'Come on, lad: be the son of your father. Let's have chapter and verse.'

'What's the use?' Thwaites asked, of no one, as if he were asking permission of the universe to make a decision. 'It's all finished. If you'll take me down to the lab, Mr Mosley—away from these people—I'll show you where the gun is.'

The next morning, Mosley was early at his official desk. Also early at theirs were Grimshaw, Marsters, the Assistant Chief—even the Chief himself.

'This is a remarkable story,' Grimshaw said, 'and he doesn't seem to want to contest it.'

Mosley looked up from a long and tortured letter he was reading. It was from a greengrocer in Lower Spritwell and it had to do with invoices, raffle-prize hampers and a sudden influx of gifts to patients in hospitals. It also had to do with instructions misunderstood by his assistant and a temporary shortage of supply. The apologies were even more elaborate than the explanations. What it all boiled down to was that owing to a series of misunderstandings, there never had been a crate of oranges.

'Before you go and lose yourself up there among the bilberries and heather, Jack,' Grimshaw said, 'would you mind getting four sacks of rotting turkeys off our backs? The Sheffield police have brought four men in overnight, also four sacks of carcases, still in their feathers, and still undrawn. Oh, and a sack or two of geese, that have been even longer deteriorating. At present they've been put out in the transport yard—hence the lack of congestion in one particular corner this morning. I gather your rustlers are playing it with buttoned lips at the moment—and asking to have Hartley Mason for their defence.'

'Which is why,' said Chief Inspector Marsters, who also seemed to have come into the room, 'I propose to take this case out of your hands, Mosley. I can't think of four sacks of turkeys as managerial crime, but one thing might lead to another, and you will not be on hand to lead it anywhere else.'

Mason was asked to come in. He took one look at the poultry-fanciers—among whom Mosley at once recognized an old friend—and said he was sorry, but he could not take them on.

'But I am claiming help under the Humberstone Foundation,' said the one Mosley knew, who seemed to provide most of the brains and eloquence of the team. 'Freddie Humberstone was my mother's cousin.'

Hartley Mason sighed, looked at the poultry-thieves with pity—and at the policeman with a sort of conspiracy.

'I am still hoping that this will not get too much publicity. Freddie Humberstone was an incorrigible but remarkably successful rascal who came and went through prison gates with sickening regularity in the forties and fifties. His wife, a patient, faithful and ever hoping woman died while he was doing his last stretch and Freddie had a *crise de conscience* in which he not only vowed to go straight evermore, but made a substantial investment, the interest on which has to be applied to the deserving dependents of men serving custodial sentences. It provides them, if not actually with luxury, at least with a few little extras. I am an executor of the scheme—an office, I might say, which is a mixed blessing. There is nothing illegal in its operation: it is a charity, albeit a highly selective one. Every case it has handled, every penny it has spent, has been faultlessly documented.

The books are audited annually. You will recognize Mrs Cryer's hand in the ledgers. I am sorry that this has come to light. If the fund were too widely known, the amount of claims on it would be an embarrassment. I have to give far too much of my time to it as it is.'

'But what about my blood relationship,' said the

spokesman-rustler. 'Doesn't that give me a prescriptive right—?'

'No, sir. Our founder was a man of some wisdom, who hoped that as many as possible of his kin would see the light earlier in life than he did himself. Therefore, in case of repeated offences, I am given discretion to withhold support from the funds. In such cases, I am always ready to compensate for over-zealous prosecutions, misapplications of the sus laws, and so on; but as far as I can I respect the recorded wishes of Frederick Lonsdale Humberstone.'

Marsters had not the grace to conceal his unhappiness. 'I suppose you can give me some proof of this so-called foundation?'

'You shall see the foundation deed. The files are copious, and it will take you a week to do them justice—but they are at your disposal.'

Marsters turned away brusquely. 'I want to see those papers, Mason: every last sheet of them. And Mosley—you'd better get down to your feathers.'

'We've met before,' Mosley said. 'On the landing of a hotel at Ember Bay. There were people on the premises who understood that you were a traveller in trawlermen's chains.'

'But there aren't any trawlers in Ember Bay,' the man said.

'There are along the coast, so you were on a safe ploy—with a reasonable excuse to stay at Bay View. What were you—some sort of messenger? Pretty small fry in the organization, I'd think.'

'Not so small that I didn't know a thing or two of what went on. Any chance of a deal, Mr Mosley?'

'Not with me, brother.'

'What about your mate?'

'What would you have to tell him?'

'A few jobs that were done in the old days. And that Mason's a bastard: picking and choosing. It never used to be like that. You could rely on the firm. Charitable foundation? Of course the books are in order. They *have*

150

to be, see? That's the cover—that's never been needed before. A few years ago there was a lot going on; and if you needed help—with a job, I mean—you knew where you could get it. That side of thing's gone to pot, since Mason took charge. Why do you think Brenda pulled out? Mason's too clever by half, makes too much noise, has too many big bloody ideas. Old Fothergill, now—you never heard much of him. He was dedicated, dead quiet. Life was different when he and his lady-love were running things. I remember being sent up to their place in the Dales once—'

'You've plenty to say, mate, that's evident. Can you prove any of it?'

'Get your pencil out.'

Mosley knocked respectfully on Marsters's door. Marsters looked over his desk, his eyes irritable and fatigued.

'What now?'

'I've struck a difficulty with these turkey people.'

'Go and tell Grimshaw about it.'

'I think it might be more up your street.'

Marsters stared at him, uncomprehending.

'What I mean is, I think you could be where you want to be by lunchtime. There's a chap down there who has it in for Mason. He'd be worth having a go at while he's still on the boil.'

Marsters cast aside the file he was squinting at. 'All right—I'll give it a try. And Mosley—from now on, stick to things that you understand.'

ABOUT THE AUTHOR

John Greenwood and his wife live in Norwich, England.

Murder, that most foul of crimes, appears to be the most British of crimes in the hands of these two Bantam authors:

From Catherine Aird:

The charm and wit that have made Aird's Detective Inspector C. D. Sloan a classic among British sleuths will draw you into the tangled webs of clues, misdeeds and intrigues that Sloan must unravel in each of these fine titles from Bantam:

☐ 25191 **HARM'S WAY** $2.95
☐ 25811 **LAST RESPECTS** $2.95
☐ 25414 **PARTING BREATH** $2.95

Look for them at your bookstore or use this handy coupon: